A Is for Apple, W Is for Witch

CATHERINE DEXTER

A Is for Apple, W Is for Witch

CATHERINE DEXTER

illustrated by Capucine Mazille

CANDLEWICK PRESS
CAMBRIDGE, MASSACHUSETTS

Text copyright © 1996 by Catherine Dexter
Illustrations copyright © 1996 by Capucine Mazille

First edition 1996

Library of Congress Cataloging-in-Publication Data

Dexter, Catherine.
A is for apple, w is for witch / Catherine Dexter ;
illustrated by Capucine Mazille. — 1st ed.
Summary: Ten-year-old Apple, who can't wait to be a witch
like her mother, tries to use a spell to teach pesky Barnaby
a lesson and gets into serious trouble.
ISBN 1-56402-541-1
[1. Witches — Fiction. 2. Magic — Fiction.]
I. Mazille, Capucine, ill. II. Title.
PZ7.D5387Aaf   1996
[Fic] — dc20   95-33658

10 9 8 7 6 5 4 3 2 1

Printed in the United States

This book was typeset in Berkeley Oldstyle.

Candlewick Press
2067 Massachusetts Avenue
Cambridge, Massachusetts 02140

A is for Amanda –
this book is for you

Chapter One

pple Olson was sitting by the kitchen window eating breakfast and looking at her reflection in the side of the toaster. Way up close she had a huge nose; from far away her neck was very, very long. Mrs. Olson hurried around making coffee and orange juice. Every now and then she went upstairs to try to wake Apple's father, who was not a morning person.

It was one of those October days that made Apple feel good all over. The sky was as blue as summer, and the smell of autumn leaves was in the air. All sorts of interesting things were starting up outside: two dogs got into a fight in the driveway; next door, baby Max Blanchard escaped into his backyard wearing nothing at all; across the street a bunch of high school kids were smoking while they waited at the bus stop. Apple watched them cup their hands around their cigarettes to hide them when they got on the bus. She wondered how they could do that without getting burned.

When she had finished her toast, she got up and opened the refrigerator and began poking through the shelves. "What's there for lunch?"

"There's some turkey for a sandwich, and grapes, and some rice crackers."

"No cookies?"

"Sorry, we're all out."

Well, it was one of those days that made Apple feel *almost* good all over.

She made a sandwich and packed it and the grapes and crackers in her lunch bag. It was a cloth lunch bag, like everybody had this year. Hers was blue and fastened with a velcro strip, and had her initials on the flap: A.W.O. That stood for Apple Webster Olson. "Webster" had been her mother's last name before she got married.

Apple found her hairbrush in the bathroom and came back out to the kitchen. She liked wearing her hair in a ponytail, now that she'd let it grow, but she was always losing her ponytail holders.

"I can't find anything but an old rubber band in here," she said, pawing through the drawer where they put things that didn't belong any-place else.

"Let me look," said her mother. She said some-thing to herself as she stirred through the stuff in the drawer. "Here we go." She held up a brand-new scrunchy: a twist of purple cloth printed with silver stars.

"Hey, it just goes with my shirt," said Apple. "Thanks!" She pulled her ponytail through it.

She put her lunch bag and her homework folder into her backpack. "Bye, Mom," she said. Her father appeared at the kitchen door in striped pajamas, his hair sticking up. He waved to her sleepily.

It was half a mile to school. All along the way

people were coming out to start their cars or pick up their newspapers or see their children off to school. Apple caught up with Sarah Whitesides just after they crossed Myrtle Street.

"Guess what?" said Sarah. "My mom's going to have this lady sew my costume for Halloween. I'm going to be a tightrope walker, with spangles all over this special leotard. And it's going to be pale blue, because that really goes with blond hair. And I'm even going to have spangles on my shoes. Slippers, actually. And a satin cape, so I can go like this—" She pressed her heels together and swept one arm out to the side.

"That's neat," said Apple, trying not to sound envious.

"What are you going to be?" asked Sarah.

"Probably a witch," said Apple.

"Weren't you that last year?"

Apple shrugged. "It's my favorite thing."

"It looks good on you," said Sarah generously.

Apple knew she was really picturing herself in her sparkling outfit.

In the science corner of the classroom Mrs. Finch was pinning up red and orange leaves ironed between pieces of waxed paper. Mrs. Finch was tall and thin and wore wonderful clothes, like purple leggings and boots. Apple had already decided she was going to be the kind of person who dressed like Mrs. Finch when she grew up.

Barnaby Thompson and Homer Brown were wrestling in the aisle like they always did right before they had to sit down.

"And then he got him like this!" Barnaby grabbed Homer around the neck.

"Aaargh!" Homer gave a huge groan and fell backward.

They scuffled and knocked into Apple's desk.

"You shoulda seen them. The whole team ran out onto the field — they had a free-for-all!"

"We're not having one in the classroom, though, are we?" said Mrs. Finch, appearing behind them. "Everyone, take your seats, please."

Barnaby sat two desks away from Apple. Whatever else happened, she hoped she'd never ever have to sit next to Barnaby.

"I'm going to be a tightrope walker for Halloween," Sarah was telling Amy Kimball. "My mom's having this lady sew my costume."

"Guess what I'm going to be?" Barnaby called out to nobody in particular.

"What, Barn?" asked Homer.

"I'm going as toxic pollution!"

All the boys laughed.

"What are you going to be?" Barnaby looked over at Apple. "How 'bout an apple?"

"I'm going to be a witch," said Apple.

"That won't be hard," said Barnaby. "All you have to do's borrow some clothes from your mother."

Apple turned red. "What's that supposed to mean?"

"Nothing!" said Barnaby with a grin.

"Class is beginning. Let's everyone turn around in our seats," said Mrs. Finch.

Apple's cheeks were burning. She leaned across her desk. "What'd you say that for?" She could hear that she sounded too serious.

Barnaby began to chant in a sing-song voice: "Your mother is a witch! Your mother is a witch!"

"Barnaby, I see you've signed up for sharing," Mrs. Finch interrupted. "If you want your turn, you have to be quiet. Now." Sharing was the first thing the fourth grade did every day. Michael Donnelly was already standing in front of the class waiting to begin.

Apple sat as still as a stone and stared at the corner of her desk, but her heart was pounding, and she didn't really hear anything Michael said. The truth was, Apple's mother *was* a witch, though nobody was supposed to know.

• • •

During recess, Apple pulled Sarah to one side. "Did you hear what Barnaby said, about my mother is a witch? Isn't that stupid?"

"Barnaby's always saying stuff like that," said Sarah.

"Your mother's so nice," Amy said to Apple. "She always lets us stay up late on sleepovers and makes popcorn and everything. Don't pay attention to him. He's just trying to make you mad."

"Right," said Apple.

At lunchtime Apple, Sarah, and Amy sat together. Apple caught Barnaby's eye as she was unrolling the top of her lunch bag. A sly grin crept across his face. She moved her chair around so that her back was to him and she didn't have to look at him, and she spread out her lunch. She unwrapped her turkey sandwich and took the grapes out of the plastic bag. The rice crackers turned out to be oatmeal chocolate-chip cookies, lots of them. She took a bite of one.

It was loaded with chocolate chips, and the cookie part was soft and chewy, exactly the way Apple liked it.

"Want some?" she asked Sarah and Amy.

"These are great," said Sarah. "Did your Mom make them?"

"I think so," said Apple. She heard a chair scrape behind her, and Barnaby came around to her desk.

"Can I have one?" he asked. "I'll trade you for some Fritos." He held out a little plastic bag of corn chips.

Apple didn't want to give Barnaby one of the cookies, but she thought if she did, maybe he'd leave her alone. "Okay." She handed him a cookie and took the bag of chips.

"Hope it's not poison!" he said as he went back to his desk.

A few kids giggled.

"I hate Barnaby," Apple said to Sarah and Amy.

"Don't let him bug you," Amy said. "He's always like that."

But Apple couldn't get her mind off what Barnaby had said. It so happened she had been thinking a lot about witches lately.

All her life Apple had been used to having a mother who was really good at fixing things. When she was very little, she didn't know all mothers weren't like that. She used to love chocolate pudding, for instance, and so there was always a dish of it at her place for dessert, even when a moment before it had been canned peaches. Even now, if they went to the ice-cream store and there was no more coffee-Oreo, her mother would sometimes say something very softly under her breath and then ask the clerk, "Could you double-check for us?" and the clerk would find that there was some coffee-Oreo left in the bottom of the tub after all. *Sometimes* her mother would do that.

But she wouldn't fix something for Apple just because Apple wanted her to. It was only when she felt like it.

A long time ago she had explained to Apple that she was a witch, but that Apple shouldn't be frightened by that word. A witch, she said, was someone who could use magic and who called up her magic by reciting spells and incantations. A witch's magic was a great gift. Most people, she said, think "witch" means a person in a black dress who cackles and does horrible deeds. But it's up to the individual witch whether she's nice to people, or mean, whether she's good or evil, and also what clothes she wears. Apple's mother herself was only a minor, neighborhood type of witch, she said. She mostly used her magic for small, everyday things.

Her mother sure didn't look like what most people think of when they think of a witch. She looked like an ordinary mother. She had short, curly hair, and for everyday clothes, she wore a turtleneck and jeans and running shoes. When she did her witch's magic, she did it quietly — and not very often. It wasn't like a full-time job.

Apple hadn't told anyone about this, though

there were times when it was hard to keep such an interesting secret. Her father said every family had things like that, things they didn't talk about with outsiders. And really, she didn't want other people to find out. Who would come to sleep over at your house if they thought your mother was a witch?

None of her friends had ever noticed anything strange about the Olsons' household. There wasn't much to notice. For a while they had had a black cat. It hadn't been very friendly; in fact, it kept entirely to itself, except for following her mother around. It would look at anyone else with flat, yellow eyes. Unfortunately, Apple's father began to sneeze the moment the black cat arrived, and no matter what her mother did — including reciting tons of spells, plus vacuuming up every last cat hair — his allergy would not let up. One day when Apple got home from school the cat was gone. "I had to give her to a friend," her mother explained.

Sometimes they had odd visitors. One afternoon last summer Apple had started to go into her mother's room when the door was closed, and she forgot to knock. Just as she opened it a crack, she saw a swirl of black: someone wearing a cape was talking to her mother right by the closet. Apple was so surprised she just stood there for a second. "Mom?" she said, and opened the door the rest of the way. But there was only her mother, rearranging the shelves.

"Who was that?" Apple had asked.

"Oh, just a friend of mine from the Midwest. She needed to borrow something," her mother had replied.

"Where'd she go?" asked Apple, looking around.

"She just left, she was in a hurry."

Apple looked over at the open window. The screen was pushed up, and the curtains blew back gently in the breeze. Her mother went on talking in a velvet voice: "You won't ever look into this closet, will you," so it wasn't a question, but a statement of fact.

A couple of times, Apple had asked if she could try a spell. Her mother always used her most serious voice to answer: "Never, under any circumstances, especially not on your own. *Never.* When you're older, when the right time comes, I'll teach you about spells." Apple wouldn't have known what words to use, anyhow, because her mother murmured the spells in so low a voice that Apple couldn't make out any words. If her mother had something really important to work on, she went down to the basement, and she closed the door behind her.

Chapter Two

hen Apple got home from school, something delicious was bubbling in the big black pot on the back of the stove. Her mother cooked everything in that pot — even pumpkin pie, even French fries. She said that was all a person needed in life: one really good pot.

"What's for dinner?" Apple asked.

"Spaghetti," said her mother.

"With meatballs?"

"Yes."

"Mmm. Yum!" Apple took her homework up to her room and left it for later. She ate some crackers and half a container of lemon yogurt and then ran out to see what was happening in the neighborhood. Sarah lived six blocks away, but some little boys lived right near Apple, and Apple often played with them. One day she'd be old enough to babysit for them.

She started playing catch with Danny Albright behind his chainlink fence. But each time she waited for Danny to throw the ball, she would hear Barnaby's voice in her head: "Your mother is a witch." She knew what Barnaby meant, and her mother wasn't that kind of witch. Or was she? Exactly what kind of a witch was her mother? For instance, what about that big black pot? Witches always came with big black pots, but in all the pictures Apple had ever seen, the witches stirred their pots over huge outdoor fires, and foul things bubbled and steamed within. Apple's mother just used hers for cooking.

Danny's softball rolled right past her.

She stooped over and picked it up and hurled it back absent-mindedly. It landed way beyond

Danny. He scrambled to pick it up and cocked his arm a few times. "You ready?" he called.

"Ready," she said.

And what did her mother do down in the basement? She wouldn't tell Apple a single thing about it. Apple had never tried to sneak around or spy on her mother. Actually, she was afraid to.

The ball hit Apple on the ankle and plopped into the grass. She looked down at it and started across the yard toward Danny's gate.

"Are you going home, Apple?" Danny asked plaintively.

"Yeah. I just remembered something. Bye, Danny."

Apple went in the back door, got her homework, brought it down to the kitchen, and spread it out on the table. Her mother was reading a magazine about plants and scribbling in the margins. Apple pretended she was doing a math problem while she secretly watched her mother. Her mother didn't do anything the least bit witchlike.

"Barnaby was so obnoxious at school today," Apple said at dinner that night. "He keeps teasing me. He says, 'Your mother is a witch,' in this horrible sing-songy voice. Boys are disgusting. Especially him. All because I said I wanted to go as a witch for Halloween. Sarah's going to be a tightrope walker. And Barnaby says he's going as toxic pollution!"

Apple's parents started to laugh. "A good choice," said Mr. Olson.

"He couldn't really know, though, could he?" asked Apple.

"I don't see how," said her mother.

"Boy would he have been surprised if I'd told him," said Apple.

"Well, we've talked about this, haven't we," said her mother in a teacherish, cautionary tone. It was the most annoying voice her mother had.

"You always say that," said Apple. She fished

a meatball from the bottom of the serving dish and placed it exactly in the center of the nest of spaghetti on her plate. "Why does it have to be a secret? If it's only witching around the house and all?"

"People love gossip," said her father. "Anything unusual, and they can't leave it alone. They have to talk about something."

"Witching involves magic," her mother said. "People nowadays are afraid of magic, or anyhow they don't understand it — there's not much of the old type around anymore — and they would probably get suspicious and maybe turn rather nasty about it."

"But why?" asked Apple. She had asked this many times before, but never got a good answer. She didn't get one now, either.

"We can talk more about it when you're older," said her mother.

"How old? Aren't I old enough now? I'm never old enough!"

"I've explained lots of times that I'll tell you

all about witching when the right time comes."

"You have your schoolwork and friends to keep you busy for now," said her father.

Apple knew he was trying to be helpful, but she wasn't patient by nature the way he was. "When will the time ever come? Can't I learn just one tiny spell?" she said.

"There's no such thing as a tiny spell," her mother said sharply, in her second most annoying voice. "Every spell is powerful."

Apple's father rested his elbows on the table. "I don't do any witching at all, and believe me, I lead a perfectly happy life," he said. "Your mother knows best. Some things can't be rushed, you know."

It didn't seem to Apple that she was rushing.

Apple lay in bed for a long time that night without falling asleep. She looked out her window and saw the full moon, silver and flat, beyond the branches of the oak tree. Did any witches nowadays ride across the face of the moon? Did her mother do that?

Apple tossed back and forth, sticking one leg out from under the quilt to cool it off and then pulling it snugly back under. She pictured herself swooping through the air, looking down on all of Abbotsville; circling over the schoolyard and the park and her friends' houses; flying over Barnaby, maybe chasing him along the sidewalk, maybe dropping a rotten egg on his head.

Barnaby was just as bad the next day. "There's this book that says witches are bald," he said to Apple as they were hanging their jackets up in their cubbies. "There's a movie of it, too. Does your mom wear a wig?"

"I've read that book," said Amy, coming to the rescue. "It says witches can smell little boys when they can't see them, and the boys smell like dog doo."

That shut Barnaby up for a while, but Apple knew it wouldn't last. Once he started on someone, he kept after them. Sometimes she felt a little bit sorry for him; it seemed like he couldn't help being awful. He was fat around his middle and pretty messy, and his sneakers were always untied and half coming off. His favorite trick was to burp at will. A lot of the boys could do this, but he was the best. He used to burp while the class was eating lunch — *burp! blup! burp!*, in different rhythms — until Mrs. Finch told him he had to go finish eating in the principal's office, and he'd have to do that for the rest of the year if she heard so much as one more burp or any other suspicious noise out of him.

During spelling, Amy invited Apple to come home with her after school to play. At lunch recess Apple telephoned her mother to make sure it was all right. But when Amy's father came to pick them up after school, he said that Amy's brothers had come home at noon with chicken pox, so they would have to play some other time. He gave Apple a ride to her house.

When she first came in, she didn't see her mother anywhere, but she noticed that the door to the basement was open. Usually she would call out right away "I'm home!" and her mother would come out from whatever she was doing and ask how Apple's day had been and did she want something to eat. But today Apple didn't do that. Instead, she walked quietly across the kitchen, and then heard her mother's voice in the basement saying something that sounded like a poem. She listened for a moment. She heard something like "ribbetty, rabbitty, noodle, something-or-other kit and caboodle," and suddenly a flash of light reflected off the stairwell walls, and she felt a *thump* under her feet, like a miniature thunderbolt.

"Mom?" Apple called in alarm. "What was that?"

"Apple? Is that you? I thought you were going to Amy's."

"I was, but her brothers got sick, so I couldn't."

"I'll be right up." There were some clanking noises and clicks, like something being locked shut, and a moment later her mother came up the stairs, turned off the basement light, and shut the door.

"What were you doing down there?" asked Apple.

"Nothing, really."

"But what was that noise?"

"Nothing, really."

"It must have been something."

"Mmm, well, it's a project I'm working on. A historical project. I'm collecting old spells and trying them out to see if they still work."

"So, did that one?"

"Yes, but it needs some fine-tuning. Some of the old spells are rather crude."

"What was it supposed to do?"

"It's a transformation spell."

"Like from what to what?"

"Well, anything you want. Chickens to mice

and back again. Sow's ear into silk purse. Those kinds of things."

"Can I watch you sometime when you try it? I wouldn't do anything except just sit there quietly."

"Spells can be very tempting. I absolutely promise you the time to teach you will come, but it isn't now."

Far in the back of Apple's mind the words danced like a faint song: **Ribbetty, rabbitty, noodle, something-or-other kit and caboodle.**

"You know, I didn't start to learn about spells and magic until I was older than you are," her mother said. "My grandmother taught me. I started with the simple ones and worked up from there. She never allowed me to try them out for real, though, until I was sixteen. But right from the start she took me with her on Halloween night. And I still love to go out and ride on a broomstick on that one night, just like we did then, and not come back till dawn."

"So you really ride on a broomstick?" Apple's

mother always said she was going to a special late party for her old friends on Halloween, kind of a reunion. Apple sensed that it wasn't her business to ask any more about it.

"Of course. I wear long johns, because it's plenty cold up there. It's just a tradition, you know, like a parade on the Fourth of July. But the real work of witching is the spells and incantations, and they can be dangerous unless the witch is carefully trained and experienced."

"Like you," said Apple.

"Like me," said her mother.

"But once you know how, then you can do spells however you want?"

"Yes, each witch is on her own."

"So how long do I have to wait before I start?" Apple could picture herself packing the lunch of her dreams every day. She would fill her closet with clothes and toys and produce bikes and skis and rollerblades from thin air. It would be just like ordering from a catalog, only quicker.

"You're ten now. I should say when you're sixteen like I was. Six more years."

"But Mom! That's so long!"

"Sorry." Her mother shrugged her shoulders cheerfully. "Look, you have to be sixteen to get your driver's license. You can't picture the street full of ten-year-olds driving cars, can you? This would be just as bad—no, a whole lot worse."

"But I'm so good at following directions. I'd do everything exactly right. And it's only me, just one ten-year-old."

"It's best to wait. Sometimes people change when they engage the power of the spirit world."

Apple's scalp prickled, and her ears got cold around the rims. What did that mean: "engage the power of the spirit world"?

"Now, I picked up some really delicious cider this afternoon at a farm stand. Want to try some?"

Apple nodded. She watched her mother pour

a glass of cider from the jug in the refrigerator. She took it and sipped it slowly.

The next day, Apple and Sarah and Amy went out to play hopscotch at morning recess. Barnaby dashed up to Apple, called out, "How's life with the old witch?" then ran away.

"Shut up, Barnaby!" Apple stamped her foot. Then she threw her rock into the wrong square. "Rats!"

"Never mind him," said Amy.

At the end of the day it was room cleanup time. "Hey, Apple! What does this remind you of?" Barnaby grabbed the broom from the teacher's closet and galloped around on it.

Apple had had it. She ran over and kicked Barnaby in the ankle. Unfortunately, Mrs. Finch was looking. She crossed the room and took Apple by the hand. "Do you and I need to have a talk?" she asked.

"If we include him," Apple said, nodding at Barnaby.

"Let's step over by my desk," said Mrs. Finch, taking Barnaby's arm. The broom clattered to the floor. Mrs. Finch sat down in her chair, and Barnaby and Apple stood on either side of her.

"I was just fooling around with the broom!" Barnaby blustered.

Mrs. Finch turned to Apple.

"He was riding on the broom to tease me, because he said . . ." She didn't want to say it now.

"Because he said . . . ?" Mrs. Finch prodded gently.

"Well, he said my mother is a witch."

"And she went and kicked me," said Barnaby. "For nothing!"

"That's not exactly nothing," Mrs. Finch said. "Still, kicking isn't appropriate behavior, is it?"

"I don't know why she got so mad!" Barnaby shook his head and tried to look mystified.

"She really walloped me. My ankle hurts so bad!"

Mrs. Finch cocked an eyebrow at Barnaby. "Let's finish cleanup," she said, getting to her feet.

Amy and Sarah were waiting for Apple. The three of them took the chalkboard erasers outside and began clapping them together.

"You shouldn't let him bother you," said Sarah. A cloud of chalk dust billowed up around her.

"He's just a silly pest," said Amy.

"You have to learn not to be so sensitive," Sarah lectured. "That's what my mom's always telling me. If he's got some kind of problem, that's his problem!"

"I think his problem is, he likes you," said Amy.

"He *likes* me?" said Apple.

When she got home from school, Apple spread out her notebook at one end of the kitchen table and settled in to do her homework. Her mother was piling clothes into a laundry basket.

"So how's your magic going today?" Apple asked in a casual voice.

"It's going fine. How come?"

"Nothing special. It's just that Barnaby keeps bothering me."

"He's definitely a nuisance, isn't he."

"Why can't you make him stop?"

"Do a witch's spell, you mean? I don't generally cast spells on people. More on things. And wouldn't it be better for you to find a way yourself to deal with him?"

"I can't think of one."

"Why don't you try laughing back at him."

"Mom, it's hard to laugh at what he says."

"Then tell him how it makes you feel."

"Maybe. But the problem is, what he says is true."

"He doesn't know that."

"Maybe."

"Now, I've got some errands I need to do. Want to come? They won't take long."

Apple thought for a moment.

"I think I'll stay here and start my homework," she said. As soon as her mother had driven off, Apple took her math out of her homework folder and did one problem so she wouldn't really be lying. Then she laid her notebook aside and headed for her parents' bedroom. She had never opened her mother's closet without asking, and it gave her a queasy feeling to do it now. The door creaked and sort of fell open by itself. The clothes hanging inside had a clean, cinnamon smell. There were her mother's familiar shirts and dresses and jackets. Apple swordfished through these and stepped into the very back of the closet. At first it was too dark to see. Then she noticed something leaning in the corner. It was a broom—not the ordinary supermarket kind, with the yellow straws all lined up together, but more like a stick with lots of twigs tied to it, and there was an empty bird's nest caught in it. On a hook beside the broom hung a piece of long black cloth. Apple spread out one edge and saw that it was a cape. The material felt funny.

38

She backed out through the clothes, her heart pounding. Up on the closet shelf was a stack of black books that looked like old photo albums. She dragged over the chair from her mother's dressing table and climbed up on it and took the books down. The first one, a book so fat it was cube-shaped, was called *The Witches' Compleat Illustrated Guide to Spells & Transformations, with Reversals also Included.* Another one, a little handbook, was called *Quickspells.* And there was a looseleaf notebook, with clippings pasted in, called *Potions for Every Season.*

Apple sat down on the bed and opened the *Compleat Guide.* She sucked in her breath. Right there were directions on how to make someone break out all over in red spots, with before and after drawings. And a few pages later came instructions on changing a dog into a cat, with a caution not to forget the meow. "A barking cat will attract notice," the book said. It was the real thing, all right.

"Apple?" said her mother. She stood in the bedroom doorway.

Chapter Three

pple jumped up, and the book toppled off her lap. "Mom! Oh!" She caught her breath as she saw that the book lying on the floor had a silver spider web engraved across its black leather binding.

Her mother folded her arms. "I guess I shouldn't be surprised. Let's go downstairs."

Apple couldn't tell if her mother was mad or what. She looked perfectly calm, but also distant, as if she had taken several steps back from Apple when she realized what Apple had done. She put the books up on her closet shelf, and Apple followed her down to the kitchen, where something was cooking — naturally — in the big black pot.

Apple sat down at one end of the kitchen table, and her mother sat down at the other. "You know, there's nothing I can do to *make* you do what is best," her mother said.

"Mmm," said Apple. She felt half scared, half embarrassed at getting caught. She stared at the salt shaker and the pepper grinder, side-by-side on a little china tray.

"Parents exist for a reason."

Apple scratched her thumbnail at a shred of something stuck to the tabletop. Way, way in the back of her mind the words of her mother's spell were playing again, like a distant soundtrack: *Ribbetty, rabbitty, noodle.*

"I always used to be able to count on you to do what was right. We've always given you plenty of freedom, encouraged you to make up your own mind."

Apple gave her mother a smile, but her lips felt thin and as if they didn't mean it. "It just looks so interesting," she said, sounding as meek as a mouse. "Have you ever made a potion?"

"I do it all the time!" snapped her mother. "And it's certainly not child's play."

"Mm-hmm." Apple's voice had dwindled to a weak hum.

"You know, if you call up a witch's powers, you must take responsibility for your own actions."

Apple felt as if she was getting farther and farther away from her mother and the lecture that didn't sound so new. She'd better act as if she were listening, like her usual self. "I wish there was such a thing as a homework spell."

"Aha!" Her mother sounded sympathetic and somewhat relieved. "Why don't you go outside and play while it's still light? You'll be more in the mood for homework when you come back in."

Apple pulled on her jacket and went outside. She didn't feel like going all the way to Sarah's. Danny was out in his yard, but she didn't want to play with him, either. She walked quickly up the sidewalk in the other direction, kicking through some leaves by a neighbor's fence. She walked as far as Prentiss Park. Apple had lived in this neighborhood ever since she was born, and she had been everywhere in the park, but she had not often gone into the very center, where there was a stand of trees. And she usually didn't go to the park alone. She looked at the trees, some with broad brown branches full of blazing yellow leaves, some with evergreen needles creating darkness. She walked a little way into the wood. It was prickly and quiet under foot. Now the regular part of the park seemed far away; even the voices of children on the seesaw had faded to nothing, though she could see their mouths working as they banged and bumped up and down. She looked above her and saw dark pine branches fanning their needles against the sky. A shadow crept out of some leaves and settled like a scarf around the base of a tree.

Apple saw a small gray rock resting in the hollow of the roots of a big tree. She looked around to make sure she was alone.

"Ribbetty, rabbitty, noodle,
I wish that rock would turn into a frog."

Her heart was thudding so hard she almost forgot to watch what was going to happen.

Nothing did. Another breeze stirred the lowest branches of the bramble bush; some little red berries quivered.

Maybe she didn't have quite the right words. She tried again.

"Ribbetty, rabbitty, noodle,
I wish that rock would please turn into a frog."

A gust of wind blew a tiny whirlwind of loose leaves into the air; it was getting darker and colder. Apple felt her spine prickle, and dust from the leaves settled into her socks. All around her she could sense tree trunks stretching up, yet closing their bark against the coming cold of night. Far beneath her feet, dying leaves pressed themselves down into a soft bed. A sharp-voiced bird let out a shriek somewhere in the wood and circled its nest in the fork of a pale, dead tree.

She was not going to give up.

Maybe the spell was supposed to rhyme.

"Ribbetty, rabbitty, bog,
Change this rock into a frog."

She did it! There was a delicate *pop!* A tiny dome of sparks lit up the hollow at the foot of the tree, and a small green frog looked up at her with yellow eyes. Then it hopped away.

"Goody!" Apple cried out loud and danced a step or two.

It was nearly dark, and as she came skipping out of the woods, she saw the children on the seesaw look over at her and then climb down and run away.

She supposed she did look funny. A couple of leaves had caught in her hair, and probably she startled them coming out of the woods that way, all by herself.

She stopped under a streetlight and looked at her watch. A quarter to six. She couldn't believe she had been gone that long. Her mother was not going to be happy.

She ran toward home. As she went along, she thought more about the frog—her frog. She wondered whether a frog that came into existence so suddenly would know how to take care of itself, especially now with the weather getting colder. Would it have a family? Well, probably a frog who comes by magic comes fully equipped. Her mother would know, of course. But asking her was definitely out.

She kept thinking about the moment of transformation, but the more she tried to remember, the more it danced away from her memory. Excitement shot all along her shoulders anyway, each time she thought of being able to do a spell. When she was a block from home, she stood still and made herself stop thinking about the frog and the moment of transformation. No more spells for now. And she had to be careful. She didn't want her mother even to begin to guess that she had tried one.

It wasn't so easy keeping it out of her mind, though. It was like having a tune stuck in her head: It came back the moment she stopped thinking thoughts.

She would do what her mother wanted her to, she promised herself; she would be a Good

Girl, with capital G's. She wouldn't cast any more spells till she was sixteen. This one was definitely it. But it seemed so dull to have all that magic and not use it.

"Where have you been? We were about to get really worried!" Her father said as he came out of the kitchen, followed by her mother. "I was going to go out looking for you," said Mr. Olson.

"I just went to the park," said Apple.

"You do need to be home by dark," said her mother. "We've talked about that."

"I wasn't the only one, Mom. There were still a couple of other kids there," said Apple. "I'll remember next time. Really."

Her mother gave her a thoughtful stare and absent-mindedly scratched her shoulder.

Chapter Four

hat night Apple went to sleep just fine, but she woke up three times with bad dreams. In the worst one, the wicked witch in *The Wizard of Oz* — the one with the cackle and the viewing ball and the evil flying monkeys — kept turning into her mother. The mean old woman, her legs churning and churning, her bicycle mounting into the air, turned toward Apple — and it was her mother. Apple woke with a gasp. It was still dark outside and she wondered how she would make it till morning.

At breakfast Apple couldn't eat more than three or four Cheerios. The rest soon sogged into mush at the bottom of her bowl.

"What's the matter? Not hungry?" asked her mother.

Apple shook her head.

"You do look a little peaked." *Pea-kid.* Apple had never heard anyone else's mother say that. She used to think it was just old-fashioned, but now she thought it was probably a witch's word. And "peaked" is probably how witches' children look. What if her mother guessed that she had done a spell? She would be as angry as the witch in the dream.

"I kept waking up last night. I had a bad dream."

"What was it?"

"I don't want to tell it."

"You don't have to." Apple's mother went to the foot of the back stairs and called, "Roger, it's seven-thirty." Then she turned and opened the refrigerator. "What do you want to put in your lunch today?"

"Anything's okay." A little sparkle lit up in the back of Apple's mind. If there wasn't anything she liked, she could fix that on her way to school. She could just fix it! A tiny spell, a really insignificant one, like for peanut-butter sand-wiches, and absolutely nothing more, was not going to hurt anybody. She began to feel better.

"All there is is leftover tuna casserole."

"Fine."

Apple's mother took away the cereal bowl. "This is pretty unappetizing. I'll put an English muffin into the toaster for you. Why don't you tell me about that bad dream? You might feel better."

Apple's father came down the stairs tying the sash on his bathrobe. "And good morning!" he boomed out. Even though he wasn't a morning person when he got up, he completely turned into one when he came downstairs. "Looks like another gorgeous day!" He inspected the weather from the kitchen window. "Morning, honey bun!" he said to Apple.

"Morning!" Apple said in a chipper voice.

"Hmm. Feeling better?" said her mother. "She had a bad dream," her mother told her father.

"It's going away now," said Apple.

"Good," said her father.

Her mother put some margarine on the English muffin, then put both halves on a clean plate and set it in front of Apple. As Apple started to eat, she imagined telling Amy and Sarah about her new spell-casting power. The next time Sarah was bragging about how great her special Halloween costume was, Apple could show her a thing or two. Come to think of it, what about Apple's Halloween costume? It was only two more weeks till Halloween night.

"Can we start getting my Halloween stuff ready pretty soon?" she asked her mother.

"Sure. Have you decided what you're going to be?"

"Yep. Witch again."

"You can try on last year's costume when you get home from school today, if I can find it in the attic. I bet it's too small." Apple's mother reached up and began to scratch her shoulder.

Apple took the uneaten half of her English muffin and wrapped it in a paper napkin. "I'm going to leave now so I can stop by Sarah's house, okay?" She gathered up her homework and stuck her lunch into her backpack.

"Well, all right. Have a nice day, dear. Hope you feel better," said her mother.

Apple turned left after four blocks and walked up Delaney Street and rang Sarah's bell. She took a couple of bites of the English muffin as she waited. It was still tasty, and a little coil of hunger sprang up in her stomach.

"Hi there!" said Sarah's mother. "Want to come in? It's still early."

"Sure."

Most people's houses are pretty much the same when it comes time to get ready for school. The kids run around looking for their shoes, and their mother tells them to hurry, and their father wanders in and out smelling of shaving lotion. But Sarah's house was quiet and orderly. Sarah and her father were sitting at the table eating waffles, and Apple could see a third place where Mrs. Whitesides had been sitting, too.

"Do you believe in witches?" Apple asked as she followed Mrs. Whitesides to the kitchen.

"Goodness, no. They're strictly for fairy tales."

"Do you think that there ever could be one *anywhere?*"

"Well I suppose *somewhere.* Maybe you'll be the first one I've met." Mrs. Whitesides laughed.

"Me?" said Apple.

"Sarah will be done in a jiff," said Mrs. Whitesides.

"I bet you'd be surprised if you found out I really was one," said Apple.

"Surprised is right," said Mrs. Whitesides. She sounded the way grownups do when they're humoring a little kid. Apple decided not to say anything else about it.

As they were getting ready to go out for recess later that morning, and Apple was reaching for her sweater on the shelf over her cubby, a familiar voice went *"Woo-woo-woo"* in her ear.

"Barnaby! Leave me alone!" She stamped her foot.

Barnaby dodged away with a hoot of laughter. Homer was waiting for him by the door to the playground. He jumped on Barnaby and they began wrestling.

"Out!" Mrs. Finch pointed toward the door. Today she had on black leggings and a big sweater and earrings that were little jack-o'-lanterns.

Apple, Amy, and Sarah stepped around the thrashing jumble of arms and legs, pushed open the door, and went out to the playground. Their favorite spot for talking was a large gray rock that was sunken into the hill at the edge of the school grounds. As she settled herself on one of its smooth places, Apple couldn't help wondering what size frog this rock would turn into.

"He's really into witches, isn't he," said Amy. "Remember when we were in kindergarten, and he teased that girl Melanie all the time?"

Sarah nodded. "It's just that he's really immature for his age. My mom says all boys are."

"Is that right?" said Amy in a mild voice. Amy had three younger brothers. "How's your costume coming?" she asked.

"I'm going to try it on this Saturday, and I got to pick out the material. It's really beautiful. Mrs. Wicker is going to make it so beautiful!" Sarah said.

"I still don't know what to be," said Amy. "Gypsy or lion."

"Gypsy's easier," said Apple.

"Lots easier," said Sarah. "I've got some gypsy earrings you could borrow, big hoops."

"Maybe," said Amy. "Uh-oh."

Barnaby and Homer and Billy Blake and Matt Peterson had started to run in a bunch toward the rock where the three girls were sitting.

"One, two, three, go!" Barnaby yelled. "Witches, witches, frog-leg stew! We're gonna put a spell on you!" They started out chanting together, but everyone except Barnaby collapsed into snickering laughter after two times of saying "witches." Homer, Billy, and Matt herded themselves backward. "Come on, Barnaby, this is stupid!" Matt called.

Apple jumped up. She was really mad. "You don't even know how to do it! You can't even do a real spell!"

"Well, maybe your mom can teach us," said Barnaby, and then he ran off, too.

"It's such a stupid thing to get hung up on," said Sarah. "Nobody's mother is a witch. If your mother was one, how could you be normal? Does your mom go around making potions?"

"What exactly's a potion?" asked Amy.

"It's like medicine, only it doesn't come in bottles," said Sarah.

After recess, they had music, and then they went outside on a science walk. The teacher gave them special pencils and they looked at a bridge and everyone drew it.

When they got back, it was nearly time for school to let out. Apple opened her desktop and screamed. A fat speckled slug was struggling across her reading folder. It was brown and glistening, and it waved around the end of itself that had two tiny feelers and then shrank up. Apple let the desk lid fall with a bang. Mrs. Finch looked cross.

"What's that?" she asked. She came over and opened the desk.

"Somebody put that slug in there," said Apple. She knew who.

Mrs. Finch took a piece of construction paper, lifted up the slug, and carried it toward the classroom door. "I'm putting this outdoors where it belongs," she said. "If one person moves while I'm gone, you're all staying in for recess until Christmas!"

Everyone froze. Through the plate-glass window they saw Mrs. Finch march outside and bend down at the foot of a shrub. A few nervous giggles came from the back row, but nobody moved. When Mrs. Finch really got tough, she meant what she said.

Mrs. Finch came back in. "A slug is not a toy," she began. "A slug is a living thing, one of Earth's creatures. Whoever played this trick, I want you to come and tell me after school. And Apple, will you please come to my desk, too, when the bell rings."

All too soon the bell rang.

Apple saw Sarah and Amy put their things into their backpacks and go out together. Amy waved timidly back at Apple. Everyone else left the room. Nobody went up to Mrs. Finch's desk to say that he had done it.

Mrs. Finch was busy with some papers on her desktop. Apple walked up the aisle and stood at one side of the teacher's desk.

"I don't know how that thing got in there," she said, her voice all high and thin.

Mrs. Finch had a neutral look on her face. Her orange earrings swung gracefully. "What exactly is going on between you and Barnaby?"

Apple kicked at the floor with the toe of her sneaker. "He's a pest," she said.

"He certainly seems to enjoy teasing you, doesn't he."

"He certainly does."

"Something about your costume for Halloween?"

"That's partly it." Apple's voice trailed away and she ducked her head. "He keeps saying my mother is a witch."

"Sometimes boys tease girls when they don't know any other way to get their attention. So then he gets encouragement to tease you more when he knows he can get a reaction," said Mrs. Finch.

Apple nodded her head.

"The best advice is, try not to take him so seriously," said Mrs. Finch.

"Okay," Apple whispered.

Inside, Apple was seething. Now Barnaby had managed to get her into trouble with her teacher, and Mrs. Finch was Apple's favorite of all the ones she had ever had. She wondered what would have happened if Mrs. Finch had decided to get to the bottom of this, the way she sometimes did. Sometimes she insisted that kids tell her everything. What would she have said if Apple had told her that her mother really was a witch?

No one had stayed late to wait for Apple, and it was lonely walking home without any friends. With every step, she felt more frustrated. Hadn't Mrs. Finch seemed rather cool when Apple said good-bye? And now that Apple was in trouble — and it wasn't even her fault — Barnaby would be all the worse. What made him be like that anyhow? How did he always get away with things?

She kicked at a rock.

"Hey, Apple!" A voice called from the block behind her. "What'd you tell Mrs. Finch?"

She let him catch up with her. If she ran, he'd probably chase her all the way home. His ears were red from the cold air, and instead of a warm jacket, he wore a ratty-looking sweatshirt.

"She knows you did it, Barnaby."

"Did what?"

"The slug."

"Oh, that. I bet she won't say anything to me. She likes me. She can't help it."

"You're supposed to go and tell her yourself."

"Why do I need to if she already knows?"

"That's what she said to do. I had to go up and talk to her."

"Mmm, maybe later." Barnaby's eyes were teasing. "Can I just ask you one little question? About your mother?"

There he went again. Sarah was right, Apple thought. Barnaby did have some kind of problem. But it was nothing compared to the problem he was about to have.

Apple had stopped in front of an empty house that had an old FOR SALE sign stuck in the ground. She noted the forklike roots of the beech tree, buried in the ground like claws. Three black crows took off from a branch and wheeled into the sky with threatening, melancholy caws. Apple suddenly sensed the beetles in the grass and knew that the eaves of the empty house were full of bats. A black cat meowed half a mile away, and the sound reached Apple's ears.

Apple's thoughts were light and rapid. A delicious feeling came over her: Now she didn't have to care about consequences. There was no one out on the street, not a single delivery truck or a nice neighbor boy raking leaves or anyone's grandmother watching everything from a front porch. Barnaby shivered, but Apple smiled and said:

"Ribbetty, rabbitty, rug,
Turn Barnaby into a slug."

Chapter Five

It was just like the rock-into-frog spell. There was a puffball of sparks about ankle-high, like baby fireworks, and when they had faded, only Barnaby's backpack lay on the sidewalk. Golly! She hadn't meant to make him disappear altogether. Then the backpack moved slightly, as if something underneath was nudging it. She lifted up the backpack, and there on the sidewalk was a three-inch-long slug.

It had to be Barnaby. There was no one else it could have been. His clothes were nowhere around; they probably went along with his regular self, wherever that had gone to.

Apple squatted down to get a closer look. "That'll teach you, Barnaby." Thank goodness there weren't any eyes. Apple didn't want him looking back at her. "You shouldn't go around making people feel bad. Or teasing them. And besides, my mother *is* a witch, and so what?"

The slug seemed to shrink. She couldn't remember if slugs had ears. A crow settled on the roof of the empty house. It stuck its beak into the air and looked down at Apple with one beady eye. Did crows eat slugs?

She better not leave Barnaby on the sidewalk.

Last year they had studied slugs in science, but Apple had not been one of the kids that actually picked the slugs up.

Maybe she could coax him onto a stick or a piece of paper and then she could carry him in her lunch bag.

A second crow landed beside the first.

Apple opened her backpack and took out her lunch bag and unrolled it. She reached into her backpack and felt through the collection of stuff that had fallen to the bottom and found a book-mark. Just the right size.

She placed it in front of Barnaby. He felt it with

his front end, but apparently he didn't care for it. He shrank into a short, fat shape and would not go aboard.

One of the crows took off from the roof and flew to a nearby tree, where it watched the sidewalk closely.

"Barnaby, come on. You have to cooperate."

Finally she scooped him onto the bookmark using a pencil. She dropped the bookmark into her lunch bag, fastened down the flap, put it all into her backpack, and pulled the drawstring shut. She picked up Barnaby's backpack, too. Then she took her time walking home.

When Apple walked in the front door, she saw last year's costume spread out on the couch: a black dress with orange pumpkin cutouts, a tall pointed hat that tied under the chin, and a dime-store broom. She walked past it and straight up to her room and took the lunch bag out and stuck it under her bed. Then she went back downstairs.

"Want to try this on?" asked her mother.

"I can't believe I was that small," said Apple. She pulled the dress over her head. Her arms stuck out of the sleeves, and the skirt stopped way above her ankle. "This thing would barely fit a slug."

"A what?" said her mother.

"Nothing."

Her mother suddenly looked alert. "It's strange, but I feel a distinct itching in my shoulder blade. You know what that means? It means there's another witch around. You didn't see anyone strange on your way home, did you?"

"There was this crow watching me," said Apple.

"I thought I felt it the other night, too," her mother added. "Maybe it was the crow. Witches can take any form they choose."

"Does it matter if there's another witch around?" It made Apple a little nervous to think that her mother might find out so soon.

"Depends on her intentions. Witches can be territorial. I know I am."

"What does that mean?"

"I like to have my neighborhood to myself. It's my territory. I don't have a big territory, but it is mine, and I want to be the only witch in it."

Apple pulled the black dress off over her head. "What happens when two witches end up in the same territory?"

"Sometimes there's a terrible fight if they both want to be the dominant witch. Things go flying through the air, curses are dredged up out of the past; that's when poltergeists are reported, and people come down with strange maladies. The witches hurl spell after spell at one another. Finally one of them is defeated, or quits fighting. Occasionally it ends in a draw — and *rarely* with a truce. Usually one witch moves away."

"Can there be more than one witch if one of them is just learning how?"

Apple's mother did not reply at first, but she gave Apple a long look.

"That's different," she said finally. "It all depends. Perhaps if they agree to let one of them be the main witch. Now, let's go to Bonnie's Buttons and pick out some fabric."

Bonnie's Buttons was full of mothers sitting on tall stools and trying to hold squirming toddlers while they turned through the pattern books. Apple couldn't think about costumes.

"How about this?" Her mother held out a corner of some plain black cotton.

"Fine," said Apple. "Anything's okay."

Mrs. Olson found a salesclerk to cut the material, and she bought silver thread and black thread and beads and something stiff to make the pointed hat. As they were waiting for their change, Mrs. Olson leaned over and whispered to Apple, "My shoulder blade is itching again. Be careful."

Apple gulped and stared straight ahead.

As soon as they got home, Apple ran upstairs to check on Barnaby. He had moved off the bookmark and worked his way up to the top of the bag and was doing fine as far as she could tell. She found an empty shoebox in the bottom of her closet, turned the lunch bag upside down over it, and shook the bag gently. Barnaby fell in with a small *plop.* She put the cover on.

What did slugs eat? She tried to remember if they were strict vegetarians. What if they only liked food that they found outdoors?

She thought of undoing the spell right then. She wondered if Barnaby would remember what had happened to him once he came back. What was it like to be a slug? Maybe he would promise never to tease her again and to leave her alone for the rest of her life. It was satisfying to imagine the scene.

She went downstairs and got a leaf of lettuce from the refrigerator and went back up to her room and dropped it in the box. She pressed the lid on firmly. He could just have a few more slug experiences before they called it quits.

But as she started downstairs again, she remembered Barnaby's mother. There were awful stories in the news about missing children. She didn't want Mrs. Thompson to be frantic with worry. She didn't think there was a Mr. Thompson either to worry along with her. And she doubted if Mrs. Thompson would enjoy seeing Barnaby now, even though he really was safe and sound.

Apple would call her up. She would tell her that Barnaby was sleeping over to finish a school project.

She tiptoed downstairs, went into the study, and gently closed the door. She took the class phone list out of the desk drawer and picked up the telephone receiver. Usually she dreaded talking to grownups on the phone, but this was different.

Wait a minute. Apple put the receiver back. Just where was her mother? Apple definitely did not want to have this conversation overheard. Far off in another part of the house Apple heard the faint creak of floorboards. She quickly picked up the phone and dialed Barnaby's number. She got the Thompsons' answering machine.

"Mrs. Thompson? This is Apple Olson. I was just calling to ask if it's okay if Barnaby sleeps over at my house, because we're working on a science project and we have to finish it and my mom doesn't mind. So you can call me later if you have any questions."

That would do it. She hung up. Then she opened the study door cautiously. Wherever her mother was, she wasn't making any noise. Apple went back up to her room and opened the shoebox to check on Barnaby. She found him all the way over on the other side at the end of a damp, glistening trail. She looked at him for a moment, even admiring the two rows of decorative brown speckles that ran down the sides of his body. She never would have thought there was anything to admire about a slug; but she had to hand it to herself, she'd created quite a nice-looking one. But had she created it? Or just exchanged Barnaby for it? Was there somewhere on the earth a slug who had just been going along on its usual trail when suddenly it popped out as a human being with arms and legs and clothes? Did it have a slug's brain or Barnaby's? Maybe this was one of those complications her mother had been talking about.

That night at the supper table Apple's mother said she had experienced a strong itching in her right shoulder blade earlier in the afternoon; it was so strong, it meant a witch was extremely close by. She might be in their house with them — perhaps invisible.

The phone rang, and Apple leaped up, knocking her fork to the floor. "I'll get it!" She raced to the study, closed the door, and grabbed up the receiver. "Hello?"

"Hello? Is this Apple Olson? This is Mrs. Thompson. I just got your message. I've just come home from work. Barnaby didn't say anything about a science project this morning."

"We just started it today. It's fine with my mom if Barnaby sleeps over."

"On a school night?"

"It's just for this one project."

"At a girl's house? That doesn't sound like Barnaby. Could I just speak to him myself?"

"He's in the basement. He's at a really important part of the experiment."

"Why don't you have him call me in a few minutes, then. Is your mother there?"

It wasn't working. She had to think of something quick. If Mrs. Thompson came over, that would be major trouble. If Apple had to change Barnaby back right away, her mother would know instantly that she'd done a spell. And what if — she hadn't thought this through to the end before — what if she had some trouble changing him back?

"Apple?" came Mrs. Thompson's voice, impatient now.

Apple's brain was flapping around, and then she thought of what to do. A spell, of course. A

73

spell would take care of it, so long as she could do one over the telephone. She even thought of a rhyme. She put her hand over the mouthpiece of the receiver and said:

"Ribbetty, rabbitty, furry,
Make Barnaby's mother not worry."

Mrs. Thompson gave a little shriek. "Oh, I just got a shock from the phone! What was I saying? Well, never mind. I'll bring his pajamas and toothbrush right over."

"No! No! Don't come! I mean, he'll be okay! He can borrow something from us. And the thing we're working on is a tremendous surprise."

"How wonderful. I'm sure you're both having a great time. I won't worry for even a moment. Good-bye!"

Apple hung up and then sank down on the sofa with relief. She hoped she wouldn't have to leave this spell on for too long. What if something awful really did happen, something besides Barnaby turning into a slug? For instance, what if the Thompsons' house started to burn down, and Mrs. Thompson just said, "Tra-la-la, I think I'll go to a movie."

Apple went back to the kitchen and sat down to wait for dessert. There was a curious silence at the table; Apple knew her parents had been talking about her.

Chapter Six

In the morning Apple got out of bed and checked on Barnaby first thing. She found him under the lettuce leaf. "Are you okay?" she asked.

As she got dressed, she thought about her plans for the day. Number one was to bring Barnaby back this afternoon. She felt a whole lot better once she had decided that. So she decided next that she was going to make herself a great lunch. She went downstairs and took her empty lunch bag out onto the back stoop. The thing about spells, she now realized, was you could do them anywhere. She saw her mother through the backdoor window, so she hurried. She barely had time for a shivery glance at the sky.

"Ribbetty, rabbitty, lookies,
Give me some huge chocolate-chip cookies."

Her mother looked up at the *pop* of the spell. Apple crammed the cookies into the lunch bag. She had thought of going on to pizza and a seedless orange, but she didn't want her mother to notice. She went back inside and sat down for breakfast.

As soon as she took her first bite of toast, she thought of Barnaby again. If her mother found the slug in Apple's room, that would be it for him. Maybe Apple should take it to school with her, keep it in her cubby. But Mrs. Finch would probably find out and decide to return the slug to nature. "You aren't planning to clean my room today or anything, are you?" Apple asked her mother.

"Not likely."

After breakfast, Apple set out for school, skipping and humming loudly to show anyone who noticed that nothing was any different today from yesterday. Sarah caught up with her, and they walked the rest of the way together. Apple didn't mention Barnaby or being teased.

She would have to act surprised when Barnaby wasn't at school. But not too surprised.

In the classroom, Homer was waiting by Barnaby's desk with a forlorn look on his face. "Guess he must be sick," Homer said, giving up as the bell rang.

"I haven't heard," said Mrs. Finch.

"That's strange, isn't it," said Apple to Amy and Sarah.

"Not especially," said Sarah.

Apple decided she better not act too interested.

As Apple was putting her sweater in her cubby, she remembered that she hadn't done her homework. She hadn't even thought about her homework—a whole page of math, her hardest subject. She had never not turned in her homework. Well, it seemed obvious what to do. It would be cheating, kind of, but she could always do all the problems herself later on, so she would get the full educational benefit.

Mrs. Finch hadn't told the class to take their seats yet, so Apple slipped the page of undone math out of her homework folder and waited until there was no one standing by the cubbies. She was hidden by a bulletin board screen that divided the cubbies from the rest of the classroom. She stood quietly, and soon a smell of ancient chalk dust came into her nose, and by themselves the dark coats and jackets rustled on their hooks.

Apple murmured,

**"Ribbetty, rabbitty, run,
Get my homework done."**

There was a puff of green sparks and a *pop.*

"What was that?" asked someone on the other side of the screen.

Apple carried her paper and folder around the screen and took her seat at her desk. Answers were filled in all over the page, and in nice handwriting, too. But when she looked closer, she saw that lots of the answers were wrong. Nine minus six was thirteen; twelve minus four was two.

She got to her feet and headed for the cubbies again.

"Apple?" said Mrs. Finch. The other kids were passing in their homework.

"Can I be excused for just a minute?" Apple asked.

She couldn't do another spell right then, with all the class listening, so she went out to the hall and next door to the bathroom. She closed the door and stood in front of the mirror. She couldn't take much time.

"Ribbetty, rabbitty, might,
Do my homework right!"

There was another *pop* and an explosion of sparks. "Ouch!" Apple snatched her hand back and the homework page sailed into the wet sink. She picked it up by one corner, sopping wet, the answers smearing.

"Apple?" Mrs. Finch knocked on the door. "Are you all right?"

"Yes, Mrs. Finch."

She was going to need just one more tiny spell to dry the page. She put it on top of the paper-towel dispenser and stood back.

"Ribbetty, rabbitty, pie,
Make my homework dry."

Twang! The spell echoed off the metal dispenser.

Mrs. Finch knocked loudly. "Apple! Come out this minute!"

"I'm coming." Apple looked over the homework. The answers had changed, but now they were worse: ten minus two was forty-seven? She crumpled up the page, threw it in the trash can, and hurried out of the bathroom.

A swirl of giggles went around the class. Mrs. Finch's eyes were on her as she took her seat.

"What were you doing in there?" whispered Sarah. "It sounded like a bomb went off."

"Nothing," said Apple.

"Are you okay? You look a little funny," whispered Amy on Apple's other side.

"Like what?"

"Your eyes look all—I don't know—sparky or something."

"My mom thought I was coming down with something. I made her let me come to school. But I have a fever. Around a hundred and four."

Amy pulled back.

At recess Amy said, "Well at least Barnaby's not around to bug you today."

Apple's stomach gave a twist. "I hope he'll be back tomorrow," she said.

"You hope he will be?" repeated Sarah.

Apple rolled her eyes, pretending she dreaded it.

"What was that noise in the bathroom?" asked Sarah. "Everybody wants to know. Did you have one of those things you throw down and it pops?"

"Yeah. My uncle sent me some." Apple swallowed hard as the lie came smoothly out.

"You're lucky Mrs. Finch didn't send you to the principal's office," said Sarah.

"I thought you hated loud noises," said Amy. "Remember at the Fourth of July picnic? You kept going like this?" She put her hands over her ears and cringed.

"Well, that was last summer," said Apple.

At lunchtime the weather was so nice that Mrs. Finch let the class go outside with whatever they had brought for dessert. Apple and Amy and Sarah sat on the bench on the far side of the basketball court. Apple's cookies had so many chocolate chips there was hardly any cookie part to hold them together.

"Gosh, where'd you get the cookies?" asked Amy.

"I made them myself," answered Apple truthfully. "Want me to give you one?"

She shouldn't do it, not with other people watching. But the heady sense that a spell was developing came over her. A pleasant, eerie humming came into the air; across the basketball court a squirrel froze in its tracks, looked at her, and ran off in the opposite direction; the swings groaned and creaked as if they were in agony; the seesaw's shadow lengthened, and beneath it something dark crouched with glowing yellow eyes.

"Sure!" said Amy.

"Close your eyes. You, too, Sarah. Keep them closed and I'll have a surprise for you."

"Why?" asked Amy.

"Because."

"I don't like stuff with my eyes shut."

"Oh, come on, just do it," said Sarah.

The two girls squeezed their eyes shut. Apple was sure they were squinting through their eyelashes, but she whispered:

"Ribbetty, rabbitty, lookies,
Make two more chocolate-chip cookies."

Sarah's eyes opened as a shower of sparks burst over the plastic bag of cookies. "Eew!" she said and scrambled back. This time there was an unfortunate whiff of rotten egg along with the puff of sparks. But the cookies — two huge circles — lay nestled in the grass, absolutely crammed with chocolate chips. They looked meltingly delicious.

"Go on," said Apple. "They're for you."

Amy and Sarah stared at them.

"What's in those?" asked Sarah.

"Nothing special. They're just extra big," said Apple. "It's only the usual stuff like they tell you on the package. Want me to take a bite first?"

"I'll try one," said Amy.

"Don't eat it!" said Sarah suspiciously.

Amy went ahead and took a cookie and bit into it. "Mmm!"

Sarah quickly picked up the other cookie and held it.

"It was just a kind of magic trick," Apple explained. She could tell Sarah wasn't going to eat the cookie, even though Apple had made it especially for her.

"Can you do it again?" asked Amy. "I want to see what you did."

Apple saw the dark thing creep out from under the seesaw.

"What was it?" Amy persisted. "What did you do?"

"I can only do it once."

"Apple, what's going on with you?" Sarah demanded. "My mom says you said something odd to her about witches. . . ." Sarah stopped in mid-sentence.

The dark shape slipped through the grass like a drift of smoke and stopped a few feet away; and then in the blink of an eye a black kitten was standing by Apple's ankle. It looked up at her and put its paw on her shoe.

"Oooo, isn't he cute?" Sarah scooped up the kitten. It let itself be cuddled in Sarah's arms, but its yellow eyes looked into Apple's face.

"I'll take it," said Apple, holding out her hands.

"That's okay. I'll carry him," said Sarah, turning around to keep the kitten out of anyone's reach.

"Who have we here?" asked Mrs. Finch when they had returned to the classroom.

"We found it on the playground," said Sarah.

"It found *me*," said Apple.

"Whatever," said Sarah with a shrug.

"You'll have to take it back out to the playground," said Mrs. Finch, "so it can find its way home." But even she looked doubtful.

"Can't we keep it for the rest of the day?" asked Sarah. "Look at how it's shaking. It needs a nice warm bed."

Homer, Matt, and Billy said "Aww!" in teasing voices, but they stood around and reached out to feel its small shoulder bones and pat its silky fur.

Mrs. Finch let Sarah put a towel into a cardboard carton and set it on the floor for the kitten. The kitten didn't stay there long, though. It stepped from the box, went over to Apple, and curled up by her foot. Mrs. Finch said to let it stay wherever it chose, because that was where it was most comfortable. The cat snuggled up against Apple's ankle and closed its eyes. Apple could feel it purring through her sock.

• • •

"It likes you the best," said Sarah at the end of school. They were getting their things from their cubbies. On the other side of the cubbies divider Apple could see Homer standing by Mrs. Finch's desk. "Want to give me his homework? I go right by his house every day," Homer was saying.

Apple hugged the kitten in the crook of one arm while she scooped up her backpack with the other. She and Sarah left the school and started up the sidewalk. The kitten wriggled free and dropped to the ground to follow them.

"It isn't fair. I made the bed for it," Sarah kept on. "It's not a nice kitten anyhow. It looks like nobody's taken care of it. It's probably got a disease. Just a stray." The kitten made a noise, as if it could understand English. "And I don't care, because I'm going over Mrs. Wicker's house today and get my costume." She kicked at the sidewalk with her shoe. "You still going as a boring old witch?"

"It's not boring."

"Same old thing every year."

"Maybe I'll change and be a tightrope walker! How would you like that?"

"Just a copycat," said Sarah, with a note of satisfaction. "Besides, yours'll only be homemade."

Apple started to walk away from Sarah as fast as she could go. Her ears were roaring, she was so mad — she heard the sound of an angry ocean and knew dark waves were hitting the sand and white foam was flying. She muttered:

"Ribbetty, rabbitty, witch's mess,
Make me a tightrope lady's dress.
Ribbetty, rabbitty, prickles and burrs,
Make it twice as nice as hers!"

There. See how Sarah liked that. Apple heard herself give a little laugh, or was it a cackle? She couldn't help it. She was getting so good at spells. She could sense the night waves still tearing at the beach, and the crashing sound still rang in her ears; but in a few moments it began to fade. She looked back and saw the kitten walking behind her. Well, if it was hers, she was going to name it. "Arthur" seemed to fit.

As she hurried along, other things crept into her mind. That was one more spell on top of the others. She hoped she wouldn't have trouble keeping track of them. At least this was one that she wouldn't need to undo.

And Barnaby! She'd almost forgotten. She hoped he hadn't starved or dried up during the day. She hadn't thought to put in anything like a wet washcloth to keep him damp. She had to hurry. She turned over different rhymes in her head, planning the spell that would release him from slug form. It would be good to take care of it before Homer got to the Thompsons' house with Barnaby's homework.

Arthur followed Apple all the way home, and when Apple reached her house, he seemed to ride right in on her shoelaces.

"Hi, Mom!"

"Apple? I'm down here in the basement. I was working on your costume. A funny thing just happened to your witch's dress."

Apple didn't say anything back; she knew

90

right away what had happened. She hadn't thought about where her tightrope walker's costume was going to get made. Guess she should have been more exact.

Her mother went on talking, her voice floating up from the basement: "You remember the other day I said I thought another witch might be around? My shoulder was itching? It started again."

Apple still didn't answer or stop to peek in the kitchen or unload her schoolbag, but went straight up to her room. She picked up the shoebox lid cautiously. The only thing beneath it was the wilted lettuce leaf with a few nibbled places.

"Barnaby!" said Apple. He was not under the leaf or anywhere in the box, nor was he clinging to the underside of the lid, or anywhere else she could see.

Arthur crouched on the end of the bed and looked at the box and meowed.

"Now what will we do? Barnaby, come on, be here!" Apple got down on her hands and knees and examined the floor and the legs of her desk chair and up underneath the bottom of her desk. With slugs, there was no telling — they could go anywhere. A whole day was long enough for a slug to really travel.

She stepped into the hall, and suddenly her ordinary-size house looked enormous, an endless labyrinth of rooms and hiding places. She could spend all day on her hands and knees searching, and meanwhile Barnaby could be inching along the bottom of the plumbing or something and not making a sound.

"Oh, no!" she said, and took a few steps this way and that. *Now wait,* she told herself. She could still undo him with a spell, even if he was lost, because he was bound to be in the house somewhere. At least then she would know where he was. But what if he had been crushed beneath her father's heavy shoe? What if he crawled across some poisonous cleaning powder under the sink? What if she wasn't quick enough, and

Arthur found him and batted him around with his paws?

> *"Ribbetty, rabbitty, toy,*
> *Change Barnaby back to a boy."*

Nothing doing. Hmm. This was turning into a problem. What if it was a fatal problem? She could turn out to be a murderess! She sternly told herself to calm down. Nothing too terrible could happen. She did have time. The slug had to be somewhere. He couldn't have vanished into thin air. Or could he?

If worst came to worst, she could always tell her mother; she was pretty sure one witch could always fix another one's spell. Still, she dreaded to think of how angry her mother would be.

Try another rhyme. She took a deep breath. Stillness crept along her bones and she could feel thumping beats far below the surface of the earth. She heard nests of hornets and wasps waking in the dark rafters of the attic and stirring in the high peak of their garage roof.

"Ribbetty, rabbitty, buzz,
Turn Barnaby back to the way he was."

She waited, straining her ears to hear Barnaby shout from some room in the house.

Still nothing.

You put a spell on him, you've got a spell on him.

The books. What about the books her mother had in her closet? Apple went across the hall into her parents' bedroom and quietly closed the door.

Her mother was still sewing in the basement, she was pretty sure, but it was hard to hear with the door shut. Just to be on the safe side, she chanted:

"Ribbetty, rabbitty, loom,
Keep my mother out of this room."

She opened the closet door and stood on tiptoe to look.

The books were gone.

She dragged the dressing-table bench over and climbed up and felt all around on the back of the shelf. Nothing.

94

She went back to her room, hoping Barnaby would have materialized under the bed. But now Arthur, who had been watching her from a fold in the quilt at the foot of her bed, seemed to spring into the air, and, in a blur of black and a whir of feathers, he changed into a black bird and landed on the door frame over her closet.

Something ominous was happening. The bird was watching her as intently as the kitten had. Her room seemed to stir with unseen life — the pencils in her pencil cup rattled, and a bunch of crayons held together by a rubber band suddenly burst apart and scattered across the floor. The room seemed darker, though Apple hadn't touched the light switch. The door creaked open.

Apple found herself crossing the room and starting down the stairs. It felt as if something was pulling her. She couldn't stop; she couldn't speed up, either. It was like walking in a deep swimming pool. The black bird flew by her shoulder, swooped down to the hallway, and disappeared around the corner. Apple kept going —

one foot, then the other. The carpeted stairs felt as if they were several inches below where her feet were landing. She reached the bottom stair and went straight ahead and then around the corner into the kitchen, where someone who looked like her mother turned slowly around from a bubbling, steaming cauldron.

The little raven flew nimbly to the top of the window frame and looked down at Apple from her mother's side of the kitchen. The gas flame beneath the cauldron hissed and glowed blue as it expanded and dwindled and expanded again. A spider the size of a baseball skittered sideways on long black legs across the polished floor. A pair of velvet black bats chased each other around the ceiling before settling out of sight beneath a cabinet.

"So," said her mother, turning to Apple. "It was you."

Chapter Seven

e what?" said Apple. The underwater feeling stopped.

"The other witch."

"I'm not a witch!" Apple sputtered. "How could I be the other witch? I mean, I haven't even done hardly anything."

"All it takes is casting a few spells. And besides, it runs in our family."

"Are you my same mother?" Apple asked.

"Of course I am." She picked up a wooden spoon with an exceptionally long handle and stirred the contents of the cauldron. A funnel of purple smoke shot up to the ceiling. "Can't you tell?"

"You look different." It had to be her mother — she had on her usual blue jeans and her face was the same face, but her expression was so different, hardly motherish at all. Her eyes sparkled deeply, and she looked as if she had been concentrating double-strength on something that had nothing to do with Apple. There was a sense of energy loose in the air around her.

"I brought you down here by the force of a spell," her mother said. "I didn't like doing it, but I knew I had to when you tried to cast a spell on me."

"I was just trying to fix something." Apple knew her voice sounded limp, and that would probably make her mother ask questions. At least the problem with Barnaby would come out. And no matter how mad her mother was at Apple, she wouldn't let any harm come to Barnaby.

"What were you trying to fix?" asked her mother.

"It wasn't my fault," Apple began. "It was Barnaby. He kept teasing me."

"And then what?"

"So I did a spell on him. I changed him into

a slug, and then I couldn't get him back. And now he's gotten lost. That's the worst part. And before that there was a rock that I turned into a frog — that was the first spell I tried — and then I made some cookies for Amy and Sarah, and also the Halloween costume, and my homework, but that didn't come out too well."

"So. Even though I warned you, you tried out some spells."

"It didn't seem like it would be that complicated."

"That's just the problem — it isn't. It's the consequences that are complicated."

"But can we work on getting Barnaby back?" Apple asked.

"What type of spell did you use?"

"It was just the 'ribbetty, rabbitty' one. I heard you saying it in the basement."

"Mmm," said her mother, not committing herself.

"So you can find him, can't you?" asked Apple.

"I can do that," said her mother. She sounded

a tiny bit fed up. "Come over here." She pulled the shiny toaster over to the edge of the counter and passed her hand through the air a couple of inches above it. In its curved side, a cloudy place appeared, and then the clouds swirled apart to reveal a small speckled slug.

"That's him!" cried Apple.

"Hold your horses," said her mother. "I'm not done yet." Slowly a patch of background came into view: a forest of long, wavy blue things.

"Here's one of your other spells," said her mother, not waiting to identify the spot. She passed her hand over the toaster again.

Sarah appeared. She looked as if she had been crying. She was holding out one side of a faded, skimpy blue costume and saying, "I thought it would be different." What could have happened? Apple hadn't done that, had she?

"Here's another one — look here," said her mother.

A frog crouched beneath a brown leaf with its eyes squeezed shut.

"Is he okay?" asked Apple.

"He looks cold," said her mother. "Looks like he needs some nice, safe mud to hibernate in. Otherwise he'll freeze to death."

The frog faded back into the swirls. Then Mrs. Olson rubbed away the smoky place with a Kleenex and pushed the toaster back into its corner.

"We didn't get to see Barnaby again," said Apple. "I couldn't really tell where he was."

"Think about it," said her mother. "If you're going to be a witch, you have to use your wits."

"I don't think I want to be one anymore."

"We'll see about that."

"Suppose I try but I can't find him? What were those funny blue things?"

Her mother shrugged.

"What if something eats him before I figure it out? Or he gets vacuumed up or squashed under a chair?"

"I told you spells were serious business," said her mother coolly.

Usually by now, when Apple was in trouble, her mother would offer to help.

"Can you undo the spell for me?" Apple asked. "I think I'm really going to need you."

"If it was your spell, then you are the only one who can undo it. That's the way it works with witches."

"Mom! You don't know how to?"

"Nope." Her mother shook her head.

"What about those books of yours? Don't they tell how to take off a spell?"

"I don't have them anymore. I took them back to the library."

"I'll go check them out again!"

"Not that library."

"Well, what'll I do?"

"You'll have to use your wits, just like I said. Now what were the words you used *exactly*? Don't say them out loud! Just think them."

Apple's head was buzzing. "I'm not sure I can remember *exactly*."

"In general, when you want to reverse a spell,

102

you say it backwards. But it has to be exactly backwards." Her mother suddenly yawned. "You work on it for a while. This witch business is exhausting. I need a rest."

She turned down the burner under the cauldron and went past Apple and upstairs into her bedroom and closed the door.

The next moment, the kitchen seemed back to its usual self. The big black pot was bubbling and sending forth a delicious smell of fried chicken.

Apple took a deep breath and slowly let it out.

Actually, her mother hadn't been all that mad.

The door to the basement still stood open. She remembered her mother calling up to her this afternoon—that something funny had happened to the witch's costume.

Apple went down to the bottom of the basement stairs. Something was glittering in the laundry corner. She caught her breath. It was beautiful. It was spectacular. It sparkled with cherry-red sequins; it shimmered with scarlet beads. First there was the leotard part, totally made of sparkles somehow stuck on the elastic, and it looked strapless, only really it had thin net shoulders that wouldn't show from a distance. Apple put it on. Then there was a cape, which billowed out as Apple turned, then hung richly from her shoulders, a waterfall of color. And there was a pair of slippers, also cherry-red. And a crown, a tiara, that curled snugly against Apple's head and stayed perfectly in place when she took a running start and did a pretty good cartwheel past the dryer.

"Boy will Sarah be mad!" Apple said. Yes! She pictured it all on an imaginary stage. First Sarah would come out, turning to show off her disappointing pale-blue outfit; then she would see Apple, gleaming grandly, and she would wilt as Apple came closer, radiating beauty and coolness. So that's why Sarah had looked so unhappy in the toaster vision. Apple's costume was twice as nice (actually it was ten times as nice), and that was because the spell had also made Sarah's costume worse.

Apple sat down on a basement step.

She guessed she really was a witch. And no matter what her mother said, she could go on doing spells as much as she wanted. She hadn't been able to put much of a spell on her mother, but what about her dad? It gave her an unexpected sad feeling to think she could boss him around with magic. And what about her friends? What would the kids say about her costume if they knew how Apple had made it? Gosh. What would Barnaby say if he found out *she* was a witch? What about Barnaby? Barnaby! She kept forgetting him.

Apple scrambled to her feet. Okay — use your wits. Blue wavy things. What was blue and wavy? What was just blue? Nothing in the kitchen . . . or the living room . . . or the study. They were all polished wood or white walls or flowered fabric. Blue, blue — the bathroom! The bathroom rug — ocean-blue cotton loops!

She raced upstairs to the bathroom and turned on the light. The bathroom rug looked squashed in places, which meant her mother had not shaken it out that day. So Barnaby had to be there still, somewhere in the rug, if the vision in the toaster was right.

Apple got down on her hands and knees and began gently combing through the thick strands of cotton. She bent them this way and that. Finally she found him, clinging to the very edge of the rug, by the shower, where the floor was still damp.

She'd have to move him to a safe place while she tried to undo the spell. She hesitated, wondering how it was going to feel. Oh well, like Mrs. Finch had said about the slug at school, he was just one of Earth's creatures.

She picked up the slug and carried him across the hall and put him in the shoebox. It didn't feel any worse than picking up a raw chicken liver, which she'd had to do once, though that had not been her favorite experience either.

"Okay, Barnaby, just a little while longer," she said. She put the shoebox top on. What if he oozed out past the top? She fastened scotch tape all around the edges, sealing the top firmly to the sides. Then she stabbed the top a few times with a ballpoint pen to make breathing holes.

Backwards. Exactly backwards.

Apple got out a piece of paper and a pencil. She didn't want to say the words out loud for fear of setting off another spell. She wrote out "*Ribbetty, rabbitty,*" then she paused. What rhyme had she used? *rug? bug? mug?* Probably *rug*, because it began with *r*. She finished writing it out:

Ribbetty, rabbitty, rug,
Turn Barnaby into a slug.

Then she wrote it out again, backwards:

Slug a into Barnaby turn,
Rug, rabbitty, ribbetty.

Then she stood up and cleared her throat and read it out loud. Nothing happened. She tried it again. Nothing.

She tried "Ribbetty, rabbitty, bug" and "Ribbetty, rabbitty, mug."

Exactly backwards, her mother had said. She was doing it exactly backwards.

After a while, Apple heard her mother come out of her bedroom and go down to the kitchen. Soon the usual five-thirty noises drifted up the stairs: plates clinking, cabinet doors opening and closing, radio music changing to the evening news.

She was going to have to leave this for later. At least Barnaby was safe for now. She was a little bit afraid to go down, though. She looked at herself in the mirror, admiring the tiara and sparkling leotard. She sat down at her desk and flipped to a new page in her spiral notebook. She wrote out the spell she had put on Mrs. Thompson as well as she could remember it:

Ribbetty, rabbitty, furry,
Make Barnaby's mother not worry.

She'd have it ready to go when she had figured out how to bring Barnaby back.

What about undoing the other spells? Maybe she didn't need to. They didn't all have consequences. The cookies didn't matter; they were eaten. And her homework was in the trash at school. That left the costume and the frog.

Apple sat thinking and doodling with her pencil. It seemed cruel to change the frog back to a rock; it probably liked being alive. She'd have to think about that.

Apple glanced sideways at herself in the mirror. She would keep the costume for now, too.

She went down to dinner in it.

"Well, what have we here? The queen of Sheba?" asked her father.

Her mother passed a plate of fried chicken and a bowl of mashed potatoes.

"It's my Halloween costume," said Apple.

"Wow!" said her father.

"I'm a tightrope walker. Sarah Whitesides's going as one, too. Only mine is better."

"Yours is certainly gorgeous," said her father. "You really outdid yourself, Harriet," he said to Apple's mother.

"It wasn't me," said Mrs. Olson.

"Oh, no?" Mr. Olson sensed that something was going on. "Well, it's very nice. Gosh, only a week till Halloween. Are you going to take it off before then?"

"Dad!" Apple gave an exasperated giggle.

Her mother didn't mention the costume. She seemed to have her mind on other things. Well, probably a witch's business was her own. Her mother certainly didn't go around poking her nose into other witches' spells. She was probably just leaving Apple alone like she would any other witch.

Apple took off the costume before bed. She folded it carefully and laid it all in a pile, with the tiara on top, on her desk chair. As she pulled on her pajamas, she remembered that she'd forgotten to do her homework again. And probably the spell on Barnaby's mother would last, but Apple thought she should call her, just to make sure. By now, the whole thought of spells made her so uneasy she decided she'd wait till tomorrow.

She went downstairs to say good night to her parents. As soon as she stepped into the living room, they stopped talking. Her father said he'd come up later and give her a kiss.

She went back upstairs and closed her door. She straightened out the tangle of bedcovers, got under the quilt, and turned off her reading light. In a moment there was a tap on her door, and her father came in. He sat down on the foot of the bed, and a complaining meow instantly sounded from under the covers.

"Arthur!" Apple said.

Her father sneezed.

The kitten picked his way across the heap of blankets and settled next to Apple's pillow.

"A house guest?" asked her father. He sneezed again.

"Can't he stay a while?" asked Apple.

"Perhaps we could take turns," said her father.

"Dad!" Apple laughed. Then she remembered Barnaby, trapped inches away in his slug shape, and she stopped laughing. "When you met Mom," she asked, "did she do spells like now? Did you know you were marrying a witch?"

"I knew," he said. "She explained all about it and showed me a few things."

"Did she ever make any mistakes?"

"Not that she told me about. When I met her, the apprenticeship stage was over."

"What's that?"

"That's when you learn a skill or a trade by working with someone who is already accomplished at whatever it is. They used to do this a lot in the old days."

Apple stared down at the hill her toes made under her quilt.

"You're worried about a mistake, aren't you," said her father.

Apple nodded. She slid out of bed and got the shoebox from her desk, took off the lid, and held it out for her father to see. Barnaby was tucked shyly in one corner.

"This was the mistake," she said.

"Well, can't you go put him back? Where did you find him?"

Apple said nothing.

"What kind of a mistake was it?" asked her father delicately.

Apple wanted to tell him, but she couldn't. The fact was too big. Maybe he could guess. She shook her head.

He gave her a pat on the shoulder. "If it's a mistake in witching, you really have to take it up with Mom," he said. "I wouldn't know what to say. With witching, you have to be born to it. Now everyone needs a good night's sleep, even witches. Even slugs. And most certainly kittens!" He grabbed a tissue from Apple's bedside table and mopped his nose. "Talk it over with your mother," he said, and he stood up and ducked out the door with a good-night wave.

Arthur yawned.

"I'm glad you're here," said Apple.

Arthur rubbed his nose with his paw.

Chapter Eight

n the morning, when Apple woke up, she found Arthur batting at the shoe-box and then backing up and making little pounces at it. She picked the cat up and put him in the hall outside her room and closed the door.

Apple went down for breakfast without much to say. "No luck yet," she began.

"Are you going to keep trying?" asked her mother.

"Of course I am!" She swallowed a few mouthfuls of cereal. "I was wondering, though, is there any kind of, you know, super spell you could use, like an anti-spell? In case I can't get him back?"

"It's remotely possible that we could summon a Grand Witch. But there's a big price to pay for that — and it's not money."

"What is it?"

"You might have to go be her servant for a certain length of time."

"*Eew!*"

"Witches can drive hard bargains."

"I'm not going to go be someone's *servant*."

"Let's hope it doesn't come to that."

Apple saw Sarah walking ahead of her on the way to school, so she called out, "Hey, wait!" When she caught up, she saw that Sarah looked gloomy.

"What's wrong?" Apple couldn't resist asking. She was going to change everything back, so what did it hurt to be a little mean? Besides, Sarah deserved it.

"What makes you think something's wrong?" said Sarah in a pinched voice.

"Did you get to try on your costume?"

Sarah pressed her lips together. "Yeah." She gave Apple a sulking look. "What do you know about it?"

"Well, nothing, it's just that you said you were going to try it on, so I just wondered if it was okay. I mean, if it was still so beautiful. Because I know you were all excited and everything." Sarah kept on pressing her lips together and didn't say anything more.

Apple glimpsed a shadow out of the corner of her eye. She hadn't noticed Arthur leaving the house, but here he was, gliding along beside her. As she stooped down to pick him up, he slithered away and leaped into the air, just like yesterday, and in a feathery blur transformed himself into a small raven.

Sarah saw it. She stopped and pointed at Arthur and turned white and then red. "Did you see that?" She edged away from Apple.

"See what?"

"Isn't that your kitten? I mean, bird?"

"Oh, that thing?" Apple gulped.

Now Arthur swooped back down by Apple's foot and turned himself back into a kitten. "For goodness' sake, make up your mind," Apple hissed at him.

Sarah ran off toward school as fast as she could go.

When Apple got to the classroom, she saw Sarah and Mrs. Finch talking in a corner. Homer and Billy and Matt stood around Homer's desk arguing about a football game.

"Hi, Apple," said Amy, who was putting her jacket into her cubby. "Cute cat."

"Hey, Apple! Where's Barnaby?" said Homer. "I called him last night, and his mother said he was sleeping over at your house. She said he was sleeping over *again*."

"She did?" said Apple.

"He never slept over at your house, did he? I mean, ever?" Homer demanded.

"I don't know where he is," said Apple with a shrug, though her heart was beating so fast it was hard to shrug smoothly. "Maybe he just told his mom that for some reason. Maybe he ran away."

Sarah was coming toward Apple with Mrs. Finch in tow. What had her mother said? Use your wits.

"I was telling Mrs. Finch," said Sarah. "You tell her yourself."

"About what?" said Apple.

"Your cat. It turned into a bird and back again, right on the sidewalk."

Apple looked down at Arthur. Now what could she say? Maybe using her wits meant saying nothing at all.

Mrs. Finch had a puzzled frown on her face.

"I tried to leave him at home but somehow he got out," Apple said, skipping the part about changing into a bird.

"It's a black magic cat, that's what!" Sarah was getting hysterical.

"Goodness, this is Halloween madness!" said Mrs. Finch, throwing up her hands. "Time to begin, class. Take your seats, please."

The class was noisy taking its seats. Some kids pretended to be vampires.

Once they were sitting down, Mrs. Finch began her speech. "Apple, you cannot bring your kitten to school. We have a rule about pets in the classroom, as you know."

"I'll lock him up for sure tomorrow," said Apple.

"You need to take him to the principal's office now. He can stay there till dismissal. But wait, don't go yet. There are some things we need to spend a few minutes talking about. This time of year we celebrate the harvest, don't we? And the change of seasons. And Halloween. Some people take the magic part of Halloween pretty seriously. For most of us, it's all pretend, isn't it?"

"Ask Apple how pretend it is," said Sarah.

Mrs. Finch went on. "Young children can get scared about ghosts or of the haunted houses that people put up at fairs around Halloween. Who here has been to a haunted house?"

Some kids raised their hands.

"Would you have gone to it if the ghosts had been real?"

"You better believe it!" said Billy Blake.

The class started to giggle. Arthur stood up and flicked his skinny tail around once. Then he hunkered down and began waving his bottom the way cats do when they're about to pounce on something. "Arthur, no," whispered Apple. She circled her arm firmly around him.

"I don't believe that," said Mrs. Finch to Billy good-naturedly. "I don't believe in ghosts, or in black magic, or in witches — but I do believe in having fun pretending about them. But we know, grownups and older kids know, that they don't exist in the real world."

Arthur rose into the air.

"See?" Sarah crowed. "I told you so!"

There was a collective shriek from the class. Something small and dark with wings aimed for a high window ledge and vanished behind the rolled-up shade.

Amy came over to Apple and stood beside her. "What was that?" she asked.

"Sort of a trick," Apple said miserably.

Homer climbed up on a chair and waved his arms. "Quiet, everybody, and I'll tell you about my personal experience with witches."

"Homer, get down," said Mrs. Finch.

Matt climbed up on his chair so he'd be as tall as Homer.

Mr. Moredock, the assistant principal, popped his head in the door. "Everything all right?"

"I'm not sure," said Mrs. Finch.

"Can we go home early?" asked Homer. There was a lull just then, and his question rang out over the class.

"*You* certainly will if you can't keep quiet," snapped Mrs. Finch. She looked shaky.

"Looked to me like it was a bat," said Apple, starting to use her wits.

"Naw. It was a kitten to begin with," said Billy.

"It's a witch's cat," said Sarah, and she looked right at Apple, as if to say, "You're the witch."

"Bats can make themselves look like other animals," said Apple.

"Let's catch it!" said Matt.

"Well, now, a bat!" said Mr. Moredock. "Just in time for Halloween, eh?"

"Whatever it was —" Mrs. Finch seemed to be recovering. "Everyone sit down, sit down right now."

"I'll call the Animal Rescue League and see what they have to say about bats," said Mr. Moredock. "Don't try to catch it if you see it again. I know they can carry rabies."

"Ugh!" said the class.

"It's a witch's cat," Sarah repeated. Apple was hoping nobody was really paying attention.

"Too bad Barnaby isn't here, he's interested in witch stuff," said Matt.

"Yeah, where is Barnaby anyhow? The last we saw of him was the day before yesterday, and he was going up the sidewalk after Apple," said Billy.

"Well, I . . . haven't seen him since then," said Apple.

"What'd you do, put a spell on him?" asked Billy. He was joking, Apple could tell that, but the question made her heart sink down to her toes.

Then Arthur did exactly the wrong thing. He popped back into kitten form right in the middle of Apple's desk. All of a sudden, there he was, sitting primly, with his tail curled around his paws, and he gave a proud *meow,* as if to say, "Look what I can do."

The class didn't scream this time, but a lot of kids caught their breath. Arthur really was hard to explain.

"She's the one with the black magic," said Sarah in a shrill voice, pointing at Apple. "Better not do anything to make her mad!"

"Sarah, that's enough," said Mrs. Finch. "Apple, take that animal out of the room. You may not be in my class with a pet. And tell Mrs. Donovan to put him in a box. Wait, I'll come with you. I need to check on whether we've heard from Barnaby's mother."

"I can take him myself!" said Apple. "I'll ask Mrs. Donovan about Barnaby."

Mrs. Finch hesitated. The class did look as if it needed a teacher right then.

"All right," said Mrs. Finch.

Apple scooped Arthur up and tried to give him a meaningful stare, but he closed his eyes and nestled his chin between his paws. Apple carried him down the corridor to the principal's office, where the school secretary, Mrs. Donovan, sat behind a pleasantly cluttered desk. Apple held out Arthur. "Mrs. Finch says will you keep him? He has to be in a box. He followed me to school this morning."

"A box? Tootsie, wootsie. Tuck him in a box?" Mrs. Donovan held Arthur up to her face: He just fit in her palms.

"He doesn't like to stay where you put him," said Apple.

"I'll keep my door shut. Maybe Mr. Car-michael can find a big box for us." She picked up her telephone to ring the custodian's office.

By the time Apple got back to the classroom, Mrs. Finch was in the middle of their math lesson. She was insisting that they do the problems and not fool around. Apple sat down, and half the kids sneaked looks at her.

"Barnaby's got chicken pox," she said.

"He had that last year!" said Homer.

Mrs. Finch raised her eyebrows and wrote something crisply in her notebook. Apple wondered if Mrs. Finch already knew she was lying. "Homer, take the next homework problem and put it on the board, then show us all the steps you took to solve it."

That was the way it stayed the rest of that day, the longest day Apple had ever spent in school. She was afraid Mrs. Finch would double-check on the chicken pox story. She was afraid to do a spell to make the kids forget what had happened. She was afraid to do anything. At first there was no one to play with at recess. It was like being in a bubble of silence. She felt all stiff and far away. Kids formed their usual playground groups, and she could tell they were talking about her and looking at her. Finally Amy came over and they got a deck of cards, sat on the bench, and played Spit.

At dismissal time Sarah grabbed her jacket and walked off with a couple of girls that Apple had never been friends with.

Apple got Arthur from Mrs. Donovan. "He slept all afternoon. There's a darling," she said as she handed him back. Apple and Amy walked a little way from school together.

"He's really a talented cat, isn't he," said Amy.

"Talented but not very smart," said Apple.

Sarah and the girls were walking slowly on the other side of the street. They kept laughing and looking over at Apple and Amy. Apple's stomach didn't feel too good.

"Is he really a cat?" asked Amy.

"I guess so," said Apple. "Was everybody saying I'm a witch?"

Amy turned down her lower lip thoughtfully. "Well, not everybody," she said.

When Apple reached home, she threw herself down on the living room couch, hoping to be discovered by her mother.

"Is that you?" her mother called out after a bit. Her voice came from the kitchen.

Apple got up and went into the kitchen. By now her stomach really felt awful. She was just plain scared. "Mom, I'm really in a mess," she said.

"I know," said her mother.

"Can you fix it?"

"It all depends. Some things are fixable, some are not. How are you coming with the slug?"

"I've tried saying the spell backwards, and it doesn't work."

"Try again."

"I already did try again."

"Try again some more. It must be that you aren't doing it exactly backwards."

Apple trudged upstairs. She pulled out the piece of paper with the backwards spell written on it and read it again. Then she got mad and yelled it out three times. Nothing doing. "Backwards! It *is* backwards, you stupid spell! Ribbetty, rabbitty, ribbetty, rabbitty! What do you want?" She held the piece of paper up to the mirror over her bureau. She saw:

Ribbetty, rabbitty, rug,
Turn Barnaby into a slug.

Well. That was something new. That was thoroughly backwards.

Her hands were trembling, but she kept the paper facing the mirror and leaned in close so she could sound out the words. She pronounced them backwards, but as if the letters were the right way around.

The next second, Barnaby lay sprawled on his back across Apple's green rug. He was snoring.

"Oh!" Apple felt so happy her spirits soared up like Arthur turning into the bird. She stood there and jumped up and down a couple of times.

Then she leaned over and shook him gently. "Barnaby."

He thrashed awake and sat up. He looked around and rubbed his hair. "Where is this? What's going on?"

"This is my room," said Apple.

"Your room? What? How'd I get here?"

"I had to carry you," said Apple.

"You *carried* me? Yuck! I don't believe it!"

"Do you remember what happened when we were walking home from school?" asked Apple.

"I remember we were standing there talking and then you said something weird, and *bonk*. Did I get hit with a baseball? Maybe we better call 911! Where's your phone? Where's you mother?"

"My mother?" asked Apple.

Barnaby blinked at her. "Now I remem" he said. Neither of them moved. "Is your r a witch?" he asked.

Apple nodded.

"Did you get her to do something t

Apple shook her head. She pointed to herself. It was a little bit like bragging. After all, she had done quite a job for someone with so little experience.

"You did it?"

Apple nodded.

"You're one, too? Let me out of here!" Barnaby shouted. He jumped up and started for Apple's bedroom door, but stopped after a few steps. "What did you do anyhow? I can't remember

vthing about it."

hanged you into something."

o what?"

eally want to know?"

do that for? Couldn't you have

better than that?"

ird was going to eat you, so

d then you got out of the

hole day, and I just now

back."

ber,"
nother

o me?"

"A whole day? You mean it's tomorrow? I've got to go! My mom'll have fits."

"She thinks we're working on a science project."

"Overnight? At a girl's house? I'm going. You better not do this again."

They looked at each other. Barnaby began to squirm.

"Then you better stop saying stuff about my mom," said Apple.

"Okay, okay. I've already stopped. And besides, listen, I'm sorry. I didn't mean to hurt your feelings, if that's what it was."

"Okay." Apple gave him a tiny smile.

"Hey, if you ever did do this again, could I get to pick what I turn into?"

"Barnaby! That's not how it works with witches!"

Barnaby ran down the stairs, and Apple heard the front door slam. She reached up on her bookshelf, got the spiral notebook, and found the words to the spell on Mrs. Thompson. She was going to straighten everything out now. She held the piece of paper up to the mirror and copied it all down and said it out loud exactly backwards. That left Sarah's costume. That had been a long rhyme, and it took a while to figure out. But finally she got it right, and the beautiful red outfit, still folded on the desk chair, vanished — in its place was a half-sewn, half-cut bundle of black cloth: her partly finished witch's dress.

"And the frog?" asked Apple's mother when she went back down to the kitchen. She must have heard what Apple had been doing, but she didn't even sympathize with her; she just pushed on to the next task like a slave driver.

"I don't want to turn him back to a stone," said Apple. "Once he's alive, shouldn't he get to stay alive?"

"I agree. He's already well started in a frog's life. What shall we do about him then? Winter's coming."

"Can you think of something? Every time I do

a spell, all these other things leak out, and then Arthur flies all around in the middle of it and screws everything up. Everyone's saying I'm a witch, and so what, they're right, but why does it have to be bad? Now I hardly have any friends."

"You still have Amy," said her mother.

"I know. She's always my friend no matter what. But everybody else is looking sideways at me and saying things."

"Well, as I said, I can't undo your spells, but I might be able to add one of my own."

Apple's mother had arranged some jars in a row on the counter. Now she began pouring out different colored powders to make a circle of tiny cones on the chopping board. "You know," she said in a calm voice, as if they were only discussing which shampoo to buy or how to catch a fly ball, "you're picking all this up much faster than I did when I was your age. I always did what my grandmother told me to do. You have more of an independent spirit; you're testing your powers out."

"I'm done testing," said Apple. "I don't even want to be a witch."

"Well, if you are one, you are one. It's something you're born with, that ability to call on supernatural powers. You can't throw it away."

"I'm not calling on them anymore."

Her mother ignored that. "Furthermore, you've gotten yourself into a fix, and I'm pleased to see you're figuring out what to do: Do what you can on your own, then go for help."

"But the way you say it, it's like a boring old rule book!" Actually, Apple still felt so relieved every time she remembered Barnaby that she wanted to run around hooting. At the same time, it made her cross to think that she was only doing what a good little witch should do.

"What comes next in the rule book is waiting till you're older to use the powers you have."

"Okay," said Apple, "even though I don't want to ever be a witch, I still promise I won't do witch's magic till I'm sixteen."

"You did say 'promise'?"

"I promise," said Apple.

"Good," said her mother. "Then I'll do what I can to remedy things. First, let's get a move on with the frog. If he has to spend another cold night outdoors, he may freeze to death."

Mrs. Olson began to mix the powders she had measured out — they were all warm earth colors: deep brown and a reddish cinnamon and a deep yellow one, and another that was the tan of ginger. Then her fingers moved very fast as she murmured something, and Apple thought she saw a small mudpie form, and then it looked like a miniature swamp, and then a flicker of jewel green drifted down into it. The next thing she knew, her mother was brushing all the powders into the trash can, and then she wiped down the chopping board with a sponge.

"Was that for the frog?" asked Apple.

"Yes," said her mother, but she didn't go into any details.

"What about all the kids at school?" asked Apple.

135

"I'll do my best. I think only a little magic is needed. Human nature will take care of the rest."

Mrs. Olson took the class list from the kitchen bulletin board and stood over by the sink saying, "Hmm." She folded the piece of paper in a fancy way and muttered something; then she unfolded the list and pinned it back to the corkboard. "That should do it."

"What'd you do?"

"Fixed it," was all she would say.

The next day was the first time Apple had ever dreaded going to school. Her mother had said she would fix things, but she hadn't said when. And what if she hadn't fixed them enough?

She saw Sarah Whitesides two blocks ahead of her. Apple slowed way down, so she wouldn't have to walk with her; but it didn't work. Sarah waited.

"Hi!" Sarah said brightly as Apple dragged up. "Guess what? Mrs. Wilkins finished my cos-

tume — she had to do some extra things to it —
and it's *so* pretty!"

"Good," said Apple.

"How's yours?"

"Not done yet."

"Mine's going to be great. It has matching
shoes! You should see them!"

Sarah went on like this until they reached
school.

"Barnaby, Apple's here! Planning another
sleepover?" called Matt.

"We did a project, so shut up," said Barnaby
cheerfully.

"That was some cat," said Homer to Apple.

"I made him stay at home today," said Apple.
She forced herself to smile, though it felt like she
was baring her teeth.

"Wonder if that bat's still here?" asked Billy
Blake.

"It wasn't a bat — it was Dracula," said another
boy with a hoot of laughter.

"I figured out what really happened," said

Timothy Magruder. "There was a little earthquake, and the cat fell into the closet, and a bird flew out."

"We didn't have any earthquake," said Matt.

"It was something supernatural," said Margaret Bailey.

"We just got through figuring out there's no such thing," said Billy Blake.

"It could have been a flying squirrel," offered one of the girls who had walked home with Sarah. "There is such a thing."

"Seagulls can fly across the ocean," said someone else.

"No, they can't," said a third person.

"Whatever it was, I'm sure it's gone now," said Mrs. Finch. "Barnaby has brought in a surprise for sharing, so let's give him our attention."

Everyone rustled around in their seats and faced forward. Something large and wrapped in newspapers sat on the floor next to Mrs. Finch's desk. Barnaby lifted it onto Mrs. Finch's desk and stood to one side. "This looks like just a bunch of dirt," he began, pulling away the newspapers with a flourish. "But it's a terrarium. You take a fish tank and put dirt in it and plants and things. And this one also has a frog, and the frog is ready to hibernate, so at recess we're going to take it out near the pond and let it go."

So that's what Apple's mother had done with the magic powders. She made a model of what she wanted to have happen, said the right words, and later on it happened in the real world. Apple already was wondering if she'd learn that spell when she was sixteen. If she even wanted to, which, of course, she wouldn't.

"That's a nice project," said Mrs. Finch. "We'll all go along with you. And we'll take pencils and sketchpads and draw what happens, and that way everyone will get some educational benefit."

Homer groaned, but everyone else liked the idea. For one thing, it meant they got to go outside for class.

• • •

"Your witch's dress is finished," said Apple's mother when she got home. It was hanging on the back of her closet door — crisp black cotton with rows of sparkling black sequins and beads down the front. When Apple took it off the hanger, she saw a spider web embroidered in gleaming silver thread across the back, and in one corner of the web a silver spider was spinning. There was the customary tall black hat with a couple of velvet ties to keep it on securely. Apple found some soft black leather boots, ankle-high, and a pair of orange-and-black-striped tights. She put everything on and spent a long time looking at herself in the full-length mirror.

"Like it?" asked Mrs. Olson.

"It's the best one I've ever had," said Apple.

Chapter Nine

alloween came on the next Thursday. Everyone was pretty wild at school, but Mrs. Finch was expecting that. They spent an hour in the afternoon playing some Halloween games that she had made up.

Amy was going to come to Apple's house, and then the two of them were going to go on to Sarah's house, and they would all three go trick-or-treating together, which is what they had always done, ever since preschool. Whatever spell Mrs. Olson had used to make the class forget about the witching had also worked to make Sarah forget about her costume's ups and downs. This year Sarah's father was going to take them, and Sarah's mother was letting her have a party afterward for everyone in her class, lasting until ten o'clock.

Apple's mother made macaroni and cheese for an early supper. Mr. Olson checked the supply of candy and put on his orange V-necked sweater. The time had changed the Sunday before, and it was already dark.

Amy's father brought her to the Olsons' door, but he couldn't come in. "I've got all three of the boys in the car," he said. Apple could see masks and plastic trick-or-treat pumpkins bobbing around in the back seat.

"Your witch's dress is so nice," Amy said. Her costume wasn't a specially made one — her mother was way too busy for that. She was wearing a too-big blouse with long sleeves and a too-long skirt that kept slipping out from a purple belt wrapped twice around her waist. She had on the hoop earrings from Sarah and a kerchief tied around her head, and she was carrying a deck of cards.

"What are you?" said Mr. Olson. "Wait a second. Let me guess." He looked at the deck of cards. "You must be a gypsy."

"Right," said Amy, looking pleased.

"Do you want some makeup?" asked Apple. "My mom just gave me some."

Mrs. Olson made up Amy's face with blush, blue eyeshadow, eyeliner, and lipstick. "You look very exotic," she told her. "I'd paint your nails, too, but there's not time for them to dry."

"I'll drive the girls over to Sarah's," offered Mr. Olson. "But first I want Amy to tell my fortune."

Amy shuffled through the cards. "You will meet a tall, dark stranger and get rich," she said.

"Good news for me," said Mr. Olson. He led them out to the car.

"Ta-da!" Of course Sarah was pirouetting around her living room and flicking her cape open and posing on the arm of the sofa, until her mother made her get down because she was leaving marks on the velvet, even in her stocking feet.

"You girls are staying for the party, aren't you?" asked Mrs. Whitesides.

"You bet!" said Amy.

By eight-thirty most people had finished their Halloween rounds and were arriving at the Whitesides' house. Apple, Amy, and Sarah had come back earlier, to make sure they were there to greet the first guests. Their trick-or-treat bags rustled with candy bars and popcorn balls and chewing gum and jawbreakers. Mrs. Whitesides had set out Halloween paper plates, cups, and napkins. There was cider to drink, and doughnuts and cupcakes with orange frosting. A metal tub sat on the floor, full of water to bob for apples, and Sarah said she had made a haunted house in her bedroom, and they were going to hear ghost stories.

Matt, Billy, and Homer came as three baseball players, and Barnaby marched in wearing a concoction of brown and gray cloth, with strange gooey patches pinned to his shirt and a fake hand colored green. He wore a sign in case somebody didn't get it: TOXIC POLLUTION.

When all the kids had come, Mr. Whitesides told them scary stories, and after that, they bobbed for apples and played Pin the Fangs on the Vampire. Barnaby stood in line behind Apple while they were waiting for their turn to Pin the Fangs.

He tapped her on the shoulder. "Nice costume," he said.

Apple just about went through the floor. She could hardly believe that Barnaby would say something nice to her, but she managed to say, "Thanks!"

When it was time for everyone to leave, Apple called her father to come pick her and Amy up. "Dad," she asked, in a low voice, "can Amy sleep over? Please? Can she call her parents from our house?"

"Well, your mother isn't here to say yes or no. I guess she can, if her parents say it's okay."

Amy's mother said it was fine, but what about her homework?

"We don't have any, Mom, remember? It's Halloween," Amy told her.

So it was all set. Apple and Amy started up to Apple's bedroom. Her father stood at the bottom of the stairs. "I'll come tuck you in after a while. I've got a pretty good mystery story that I can't wait to finish."

"Come on, Amy." Apple led her into the bedroom and took an extra pair of pajamas out of her bureau drawer. They put on their nightclothes, brushed their teeth, and got into bed.

"Do you want something to read?" asked Apple.

"Sure," said Amy. "Have you got any ghost stories?"

Apple pulled out *Tales to Give Your Goosebumps Goosebumps* and opened it to the first page.

"Wait a minute," said Amy. "I'm going to have just one more piece of candy. I can always brush my teeth again."

"Okay. Me too."

They each had four more pieces while Arthur paced across the rug, lashing his tail from side to side. Every now and then his fur stood on end and he jumped into the air, arched his back, and screeched, "*Meow!*"

"Let's turn out the light and read with a flashlight," said Apple.

"Okay!" Amy squealed and pulled the quilt up to her nose.

Apple got out of bed and rummaged through her desk drawer and pulled out her camp flashlight. Then she hopped back under the covers and switched off the bedside light. She waited a moment for the full effect of the blackness. You could not see a thing.

"Are you going to turn on the flashlight?" Amy's voice dropped to a whisper.

Something rattled against the window.

"What was that?" asked Amy.

Apple put the flashlight under the covers and got out of bed. She went over to the window and pulled back the shade. Folds of dark cloth whirled and rippled by the glass, and then a face came close up, smiling beneath a black-brimmed hat. Apple's mother knocked on the window pane. She was bouncing around as the wind tossed the broomstick up and down. Apple pushed up the window.

"Would you two like to come for a ride?" asked her mother.

"On that?"

"Find some sweaters and sweatpants to keep you warm."

"Is that your mother?" asked Amy, huddling behind Apple. "Is she in a tree?"

"She says she'll take us for a ride. Want to?"

Amy's eyes were huge. "I don't know . . . Maybe I better ask my mom."

"I wouldn't," advised Mrs. Olson. "Come along, unless you're scared of heights. I promise you it's safe."

Apple pawed through her closet for some long fleece pants and a couple of jackets.

"Let's put Amy on first, because she's smaller," said Mrs. Olson.

"Ooop!" Amy let out one squeak as Apple helped her up onto the windowsill. She took Mrs. Olson's hand and hopped across to the broomstick.

"Hang on to my waist, like on a toboggan," said Apple's mother.

Amy hugged her and hung on for dear life.

Now Apple stepped up on the sill. Her mother reached out and took her hand, and Apple leaped across the gap and landed in place behind Amy. She clutched Amy around the waist. Arthur gave a *rowl* and fastened on to the broom-straws, and they were off.

Apple was afraid to look at first — the wind was in her face and ears, and she could tell they were going up, up. The broomstick was so nar-row Apple couldn't see why she didn't slip off it, but something, maybe their forward momentum, made her feel securely balanced. She turned around to check on Arthur. He was hanging on, his claws dug into the twigs, his ears flat back, and his eyes squinting in the wind.

Then the rush of air died away, and Apple opened her eyes in the quiet. Above them the harvest moon shone fat and full. Below, Apple saw all of Abbotsville: its streets and streetlights, its houses, the park with the mysterious woods, and their school. They floated over driveways, highways, railroad tracks — twin lines of silver racing to the west — and the dark path of a river.

They passed high above a man bundled up in a jacket and scarf, out late walking his dog. They left a whistle of cold air about his ears and an echo in the sky. The man stopped and looked cautiously about him, then called his dog in close and turned for home.

Now the broomstick headed upward again, and they flew out over the countryside. Apple saw farmers' fields full of pale cornstalks and unsold pumpkins. There was a farmhouse with a pair of carved pumpkins on its front porch — one frowning, one smiling, with pointed teeth and eyebrows carved into the thick orange shell, and a candle still flickering inside each one. A ghost made of a sheet billowed in a nearby tree. A scrappy dog in the yard barked up at them, and Arthur answered with a hiss. Apple wondered if a child looking out his window could see them — a trio plus a cat, silhouetted against the moon. She waved down, just in case.

They flew on until they were among mountains, whose steep sides were covered with pine and spruce trees. Ahead of them rose the tallest peaks, bare rock already streaked with snow. Apple's mother flew between the two tallest peaks.

Now Apple began to see other witches flying around: first one, then a group of five, then some creatures that seemed to be animals that didn't ordinarily have wings but did now.

"Do we have to stay here long?" Apple asked uneasily.

Amy's head rested on Mrs. Olson's back; she had gone to sleep.

"I never stay longer than just to say hello," said Apple's mother. "There are all sorts of spirits here — some you wouldn't want in your house — but I want to stay on speaking terms with them."

They circled over a gathering of . . . what were they? Apple both did and did not want to look. So she looked. There were ghosts, faded and sad-looking, and ghosts that looked mischievous. There were witches, dozens of witches — some mean-looking, some crafty-looking, some just disheveled; some were handsome, some were homely; some looked strong, some were lying like limp scarecrows on the ground. A few small ones, probably goblins, crouched over fires and sang. The mother of all cauldrons, a pot as big as the Olsons' whole stove, sat over a burning fire. The place was swarming with bats and black cats and lizards and spiders and toads slithering in and out of the smoke and fog.

The broomstick hovered a few feet above the

ground. A ghost drifted up beside Apple and hung there, treading air.

"Let me do the talking," whispered her mother. "Evening, ladies!" she sang out.

"Harriet! It's Harriet! How have you been? Come down. Have some little ones with you, do you? Set them down with us for a visit!" Cackles and cries of welcome rippled through the crowd.

"Yes, set your broom down here with us for a while! Hee-hee-hee!"

"Not tonight," said Apple's mother firmly. "We've got too far to go. But good health to you all!"

"And to you, too, dearie!"

Various voices called up to them.

"May good fortune follow you!"

"May your powers stay strong!"

"Live long and prosper!" said somebody.

"Shut up," said somebody else crossly.

"Oh yes, she's got too far to go. She always says that," complained one witch.

"Hurry, Mom," said Apple.

They flew away and higher until the mountains themselves looked small, like the models kids make in school. They flew beside a monstrous thundercloud as big as a city block, with lightning flashing and thunder exploding all through it.

At last they were so high that all around them was nothing but deep sky, transparent and black, and the light from a million stars.

And then they began to descend. Somewhere around skyscraper level Apple fell asleep. She felt herself gently circling lower, and she took one last peek at the sleeping world — dark houses, empty streets, quiet birds, bats, the ordinary kind, hunting for insects, owls hunting for field mice, field mice staying in their underground tunnels if they were smart.

Apple saw a hint of greenish light come across the horizon. Halloween was over.

"I had the most amazing dream last night!" said

Amy. She sat up. She was sleeping in Apple's trundle bed, which took up all the rest of the space in the room when it was pulled out.

"What time is it?" asked Apple. She turned over and looked across her pillow to her alarm clock. Arthur, curled in a ball at the foot of her bed, did not stir. "Seven-thirty! Oh, no. We better get going."

"Want to hear about my dream?" asked Amy.

"Sure," said Apple.

She listened to Amy as they pulled on their clothes and straggled downstairs. Apple's father stood by the stove with a striped apron tied around his middle. "Your mother's sleeping in," he said. "What would you like for breakfast? I can make a fast omelet, or we've got some pancake mix, or there's toast."

"Omelets! Pancakes!" they said.

"Hope you're hungry," said Mr. Olson.

They seated themselves at the table.

"Dad, did you tuck me in last night?" asked Apple. "I can't remember."

"You were asleep, but I did say good night and tucked in your quilt. I did yours, too, Amy."

"I was telling Apple all about the dream I had last night. I dreamed I went riding with a witch all around on Halloween."

"I had the same one!" said Apple. She and her father exchanged looks.

"I wonder how much you'll get done in school today," Mr. Olson said, flipping the first omelet over. Melting cheese sizzled as it hit the bottom of the pan.

"Not much. Everybody'll be on a sugar high," said Amy.

"Oh, Mrs. Finch will think up something for us . . ." said Apple.

"So we'll get the full educational benefit!" both girls said at once.

"November first is one day I'm glad I'm not a grade-school teacher," said Mr. Olson with a chuckle.

"Remember the party?" said Amy. "Barnaby

looked so funny. And it was too bad when Sarah did a somersault and her shoes flew into the apple-bobbing tub! And remember afterward, when we came here . . . and . . . well, hey, now I'm wondering. Did I dream all that or did it happen?" She watched her plate as Mr. Olson slipped the omelet onto it. Then he cut the omelet down the middle and gave half to Apple.

"I think it happened," said Apple.

"I don't think it could have," said Amy confidently. "Anyways, I'm kind of glad Halloween is over. I wonder if my brothers got as much candy as I did. Next week I bet we have to start studying pilgrims and turkeys. I'm so glad you asked me to sleep over."

"We had a good time, didn't we," said Apple.

They finished their breakfast. It had turned sharply colder sometime during the night, and a strong wind was blowing the rest of the leaves from the trees. Apple lent Amy one of her old jackets, and they ran to catch up with Sarah on the other side of Myrtle Street. Then the three of them kicked through the gutters on their way to school, scattering leaves and Halloween scraps, racing each other all the way.